HOLD YOUR FIRE

CHLOE WILSON

SCRIBNER

LONDON NEW YORK SYDNEY TORONTO NEW DELHI

First published in Australia in 2021 by Scribner, an imprint of
Simon & Schuster (Australia) Pty Limited

First published in Great Britain by Simon & Schuster UK Ltd, 2024

1 3 5 7 9 10 8 6 4 2

Simon & Schuster UK Ltd
1st Floor
222 Gray's Inn Road
London WC1X 8HB

Simon & Schuster Australia, Sydney
Simon & Schuster India, New Delhi

Simon & Schuster: Celebrating 100 Years of Publishing in 2024

www.simonandschuster.co.uk
www.simonandschuster.com.au
www.simonandschuster.co.in

A CIP catalogue record for this book
is available from the British Library

Paperback ISBN: 978-1-3985-3676-0
eBook ISBN: 978-1-3985-3677-7

This book is a work of fiction. Names, characters, places and incidents are
either a product of the author's imagination or are used fictitiously. Any resemblance
to actual people living or dead, events or locales is entirely coincidental.

Jacket art by Joy Hester
Jacket design by Katie Forrest

Printed and Bound in the UK using 100% Renewable
Electricity at CPI Group (UK) Ltd

Contents

The Leopard Next Door

My neighbour bought a leopard. He bought it when it was eight days old. He said it tried to roar and sounded like a bird.

He had to bottle-feed the leopard every few hours. It's like having a baby, he said: getting up in the night, wrapping the little body in a blanket, and waiting for it to relax and become dead weight in your arms. I asked if I could pay the leopard a visit. He said there was too much risk I'd pass on a disease.

It seems relevant to mention that we lived on the ninth floor of an apartment block. The carpark was a popular location for drug deals, and a body had once been dumped in the lane that separated our building from the next. Real estate agents always claimed that this part of town was 'going places'. Going where, I wondered.

I saw my neighbour almost every day in the months after he brought the leopard home. His beard grew out, and a faint, pissy smell wafted from his clothing.

'How's the leopard?' I'd ask. He'd answer in one-word descriptions: 'restless', 'irritable'. Once he said 'depressed', and I imagined the juvenile leopard sulking on my neighbour's couch, watching re-runs in the dark.

Then I didn't see my neighbour anymore.

I began to worry. I knocked on his door. I knocked for three days in a row, calling, 'Hello? Hello? Is anyone there?'

That third day, I saw a shadow pass in the gap between the door and the carpet, and heard a noise, muffled, a sort of *wumph* – like someone sliding down a wall and slumping on the floor.

My neighbour had given me a spare key, in case of emergencies. The following day, I used it – I threw a raw steak into his hallway, and slid a bucket filled with water in after it. Then I slammed the door.

I did the same thing the next day, and the next. And we went on like this. Because something kept taking my offerings, and something kept *wumph*ing and shuffling and pacing in that apartment.

Maybe I should have called the police. But I didn't want to get my neighbour into trouble. Besides, I liked the idea of having a leopard next door – someone who stayed up nights, like me; someone else who knew they were in the wrong place but didn't know how to get out.

Tongue-Tied

I knew it was her before she turned around. Gym teachers, unlike other teachers, don't know their students seated and face-forward. We know their proportions, their ratio of muscle to fat, the smell of their feet, of their unwashed groins and underarms. We know their limits.

'Shit,' I said. As we pulled in behind the tiny hatchback, I looked closely at the real estate agent with whom we'd be spending an idle, aspirational afternoon. She was standing on the pavement. Hearing our approach, she turned, smiling at no-one and hugging a clipboard to her chest. A mauve silk scarf was knotted around her neck. When she took a step towards our car, its tails blew into her face.

'What?' Pete asked from the driver's seat. He was looking at himself in the rear-view mirror, pulling up a nostril to check his nose hairs. He had a small electric trimmer – a smooth, tapered thing like a bottom-feeding fish – for the express purpose of keeping them in check. He'd let it nibble away at him that morning, but the bright light in the car revealed the hairs he'd missed.

'I know her,' I said. 'She was a student.'

Pete grasped an untrimmed hair between his thumb and forefinger and yanked. He grimaced, tears in his eyes, then inspected the end to make sure he'd ripped the root out.

Meanwhile she waited. Cilla Jones, with the same slight bow in her legs, the same bulge at the back of her skull. I felt a weird thrill, the way you might feel about seeing an ex-lover unexpectedly: that quiver down to the bowels, the rush that is equal parts excitement and dread.

Pete blinked away the tears. 'Was she a loser?'

'Worse.'

'Worse?' He sniffed hard and twisted the mirror back into place. 'How does it get worse?'

'She was … pathetic.'

There would be no avoiding Cilla's company. This excursion had been arranged for us by the real estate agency, after we'd told them we were only interested in homes available for private sale. Pete had an aversion to games of chance, and this extended to auctions. The agency had agreed to send someone to show us around.

I wondered whether Cilla would be as shocked to see me as I was to see her.

I set my face into a teacher's practised blankness and stepped out into the day's strange weather – overcast, with white glare and intermittent blasts of dusty wind. I instinctively drew myself up to my full athlete's height, sucking my navel towards my spine, rolling my weight from my heels to the balls of my feet.

Did she recognise me? She took a few tottering steps forward in her kitten heels to slip her small, hot hand into the hand I had extended. If she did know me she didn't flinch.

'Hiya,' she said. 'I'm Priscilla from George Jones Real Estate. I'll be showing you folks around today.'

Hiya. Folks. A rehearsed line, a new name, another uniform: the company's charcoal suit and natty mauve scarf. But it was definitely her. The company must have been her father's, which would explain the mystery of how she'd acquired a job at all. As soon as she spoke I remembered her voice: like a baby's voice, breathy, dropping letters from her words. I remembered wondering whether it was an attempt to be cute, that voice, or worse – an attempt to be sexy. It rankled when I taught her; it rankled with me now.

Pete was already narrowing his eyes, scrutinising her.

'You must be Mr Ford,' she said. She closed her mouth and smiled with it and let her gaze drift back to me.

Cilla wasn't stupid, exactly, and nor was she ugly. There were plenty of ugly, stupid girls who got through their schooldays just fine. Cilla was off. She had a musty smell, like a forgotten shoe dusted with mildew. She played the recorder, an instrument that everyone else – including the music teachers – regarded as a toy. She did nothing to extract or conceal the whiteheads that mushroomed along her hairline.

But the school, a private girls' school, was genteel. No-one was openly unkind to Cilla, no-one called her names. Instead, stories circulated: she had let a tampon rot inside her and nearly died of toxic shock. She had licked a kidney that she was supposed to be dissecting. And so she seemed not only odd, but unclean, possibly contagious, and the other girls avoided her with the instinct that makes herd animals avoid any of their number too sick or small or deformed to survive. I didn't blame them. I felt it too, the urge to take a step back from her, to try not to breathe in the air she exhaled, or touch her hand or her hair by accident.

And here I was, shaking that hand, trying to ignore the desire I felt to wipe my palm on my jeans.

A quick assessment told me that in the decade since I'd seen her she had grown taller, but not by much; had filled out, but not by much. Her bra was slack, and she had the loose-fleshed look of someone who does nothing to maintain their muscle tone.

If this sounds cruel, I suppose it's because what they say about gym teachers is true: we are cruel. Had I felt a certain pleasure seeing someone pitch a ball into Cilla's doughy, unformed body? Did I enjoy watching her noodly arms shake as they tried and failed to climb a rope? Yes, and yes. But I was not motivated by a particular sadism towards Cilla. I was angry with any girl who couldn't wheeze her way through a single lap, or complete an entire push-up.

I was angry because I was also proof of that other cliché: those who can't, teach. How well I remember being on the lacrosse pitch that day. I remember running after a girl, her long dark ponytail swishing ahead of me, the fat on her thighs vibrating each time her foot slammed into the turf. She stopped, so I stopped, and there was a sound – a factual little pop. I dropped to the grass. That was it; that was the end.

Now I was a teacher, and Pete was a nurse, and one thing we had in common was a shared bitterness about our careers – specifically, the paltriness of our salaries. This was why we had been considering a move to the country. We regularly discussed the subject of money, and how ours would 'go further' in a country town. Each of these conversations was tinged with the desperate sniffing-out-of-scraps that phrase implies.

'People have died in my arms, Amy,' Pete would say sometimes, chopping a cucumber or meticulously towelling between his toes. 'I mean, if that's not worth something, what is?'

I'd known, or at least I remembered knowing, that Cilla was from the country. I had imagined it must be somewhere tiny, fragile, hidden. A grotto, a dell, the kind of place that could spawn someone like her. I hadn't thought of her being from a place like this.

The town was almost a city: too big to be charming, too small to be cosmopolitan. Its historical buildings were surrounded by larger, more recent developments, and the whole was encircled by an industrial fringe: a carpet manufacturer miraculously still in business, a fan-belt factory that wasn't. We drove past empty storefronts, lower-end chain stores, bars that promised both topless waitresses and $6.95 earlybird specials.

But this town needed teachers, and nurses, and the government was willing to pay a little extra to lure them from the city. We could make a nice life here, Pete had said. And wasn't that what we wanted? To have a nice life?

At the first house, Pete jammed his hands in his pockets. He was wearing shorts, despite the weather, as though he needed to prove something to the cold.

Cilla held up the key. 'Shall we?' she said.

We followed her along the path to the front door and I took in her too-jaunty walk, as confident as it was lopsided, with one hip rotating up and forward. I pictured the ball rolling in that socket. It set my teeth on edge.

The first house was also the cheapest. It spread to the edges of a wide block, and was dated, beige, with a garden made from jagged stones and huge, hostile yucca plants. The whole house seemed to be hunching low to the ground. As Cilla slipped the key into the lock she turned, and must have caught my expression.

'It's nicer inside,' she said, and flushed beneath the powder she wore, which had settled on the blonde hair fuzzing her cheeks.

Cilla hadn't lied, exactly. The house was nicer inside. But it had the thin, held-breath confidence of someone trying to get away with something. The bright throw cushions, the tall vase of flowers on the dining table; these details directed by an expert hand couldn't hide how obsessively utilitarian everything else felt. The surfaces were clean, but what was most remarkable about them was how wipeable they were: everything was laminate or the kind of broad white tile you might find in an operating theatre. The place seemed designed to withstand regular hosing-down.

I tried to imagine who had lived here, who had designed their life around avoiding stains or bacteria, or living with any fixture that required care to be taken.

'I think I've seen enough,' I said.

But Pete was still looking. There was something that had captured his imagination: the security features. When Cilla showed him the alarm, CCTV, motion sensors and security light, he nodded in satisfaction, perhaps recognising in the hoser-downer a kind of kindred spirit. Pete loved security, not because he felt threatened by any imminent danger, but because he disliked the idea of someone getting the better of him. He didn't even walk away when he was grilling chicken. He would crouch down and watch, taut as a guard dog, in case the wavering blue flame behaved unpredictably once his back was turned.

The only other extravagance in the first house were the lights, which could be switched on and off by clapping. Cilla demonstrated, or tried to; her hands connected but the sound failed to resonate. Pete clapped loudly and the lights vanished; he clapped again and they came on.

But once wasn't enough for him. He stood in the bare, tiled living room and clapped his hands again and again, making the light appear and disappear.

'Just testing its reflexes,' he said, smiling at Cilla.

Cilla swayed on the spot as if she was about to dance and gave a breathy little laugh.

'Would you like to move on to the next house?' she said.

Pete clapped. On. Off. On. Off.

Cilla made a show of taking her phone out, exclaiming at the time.

'This is fun,' Pete said, looking at me. 'Isn't it?'

'I guess,' I said.

He clapped once more and the lights flicked off.

On the way back to our cars, I saw Cilla work a handkerchief – a tightly folded white square – out of her sleeve. While she thought she was unobserved, she dabbed at the corners of her mouth. Another memory surfaced: Cilla and her handkerchiefs. I recalled a day when her class was doing a gymnastic circuit. At one station, students had to perform a rudimentary hang on the uneven bars. Cilla had no hope of holding up her own weight. Her muscles started shuddering almost instantly, even while I held my palm against the knobs of her spine.

I remembered her handkerchief dropping from her pocket to the floor, and I remembered how quickly she detached from that bar to retrieve it, how lightly she landed. She gathered the handkerchief and scurried off the mat. It was the most agile sequence of movement I ever saw her make.

In the car Pete sniffed.

'I see what you mean,' he said.

'About what?'

'That woman. She's not right. She has a real shit-eating grin.'

At that point, I thought to tell Pete the story of the poo phantom.

It happened when Cilla was in year eight. Rumours about the first incident spread with that invisible, light-speed energy they have in a school: all at once, everyone knew that someone in the D-building restrooms had, after hours, written a message in shit on the walls. A week later it happened again and an assembly was called. The vice-principal – a tall undertaker of a man who wore faded colours and had a loose, low-hanging paunch – stood on stage and through a series of euphemisms asked the perpetrator to seek help, promising complete confidentiality.

After the assembly, I asked one of the other teachers what the messages were.

'The first said *Hi*,' she told me. 'And the second said *Help*.'

'Oh,' I said. 'That's all?'

My colleague gave me a wry look.

'I guess she had to keep it short,' she said.

Suspicion took a while to fall on Cilla, but when it did, it stuck. We never knew for sure that it was her, but as far as the other girls were concerned, she still had shit on her hands. At the end of that term she vanished. And once she was gone, she wasn't missed.

I almost told Pete this story, but something stopped me. From early on I had understood that ours would not be a relationship of gradually communicating our strangenesses, our weaknesses, our undignified moments, to one another. He had, for instance, never once passed gas in my presence. I don't know how I became aware of this, but it resulted in my feeling that I shouldn't pass gas in his presence, either. This was a discipline I now rigorously observed. There had been nights when I woke myself up either by passing gas or having a vivid nightmare in which I did, and then lay there with my heart racing, hoping he hadn't heard.

He would not, I decided, appreciate the story of the poo phantom. And I didn't want the shame of what Cilla had done – what she might have done – to stick to me.

What had attracted me to Pete in the beginning? Looking at him, his eyes trained with ferocious concentration on Cilla's hapless, apologetic hatchback, I felt both drawn to him and repulsed by him. I liked his certainty, his untroubled conscience, his sense of purpose. He was someone who woke up before the alarm and then took pleasure in switching it off. He often asked to speak to the manager. He would not allow strong-smelling foods into our apartment – no anchovies, no curry powder, no blue cheese. I knew that these were irritating traits. And yet I admired them, saw something heroic in them, the way you might think it heroic for someone to fight a wildfire with a water pistol.

I met Pete when he was the nurse at my local doctor's clinic. I was there because I needed a series of antibody injections. Specifically, rabies antibody injections.

When the clinic said I had to make an appointment with the nurse, I pictured a woman with middle-aged spread in shoes with solid arch support. Not this tall, healthy man with a face that managed to be boyish and pious at once.

'You haven't noticed any symptoms?' he said.

'No … ?'

'No thirst, sweating?'

I shook my head.

'You're not foaming at the mouth?' He smiled, pleased at his joke.

'Not yet,' I said.

He retrieved a refrigerated bag and withdrew the vaccine, then began assembling the things he'd need, each wrapped in its own sterilised package.

'Dog bite?' he asked, confident, peeling the packaging away. I could see that his abdomen was a flat, disciplined plane, and I had an athlete's appreciation for the denial that had gone into its making.

I smiled. 'Bat.'

That got his attention.

'A bat? Seriously?'

'Seriously.'

'Show me.'

I was charmed by his enthusiasm for my wound. I showed him my hand – the small but deep impressions left by the bat's fangs.

'So you're a vampire now?' he asked. 'Feeding on the blood of the living?'

I gave a weak laugh, watched him tip the tiny glass bottle upside down and pull the plunger back.

'How did it happen?'

'It was so stupid,' I said.

I told Pete the story: it had been a hot night in February. I walked into my stuffy, low-ceilinged apartment and opened the window. Immediately – before I could switch on the light, before I had even turned around, it flew in. At first I thought it was a moth. It had a moth's lightness, and the frantic jagging of its body in circles around the ceiling suggested a moth's weight, a moth's panic. I went to wave it away. When I realised what it was I pulled my hands back like I'd received an electric shock.

'Then what?'

He came towards me holding the uncapped syringe.

'I got a lacrosse net. I tried to catch it. It got tangled in the net, and when I went to let it go, it bit me.'

'You play lacrosse?'

'Not anymore.'

He swabbed my upper arm and then, with no preamble, stuck the needle in. I didn't wince. I braced my core and breathed through it. The rabies vaccine is a painful one. I felt the crawl of the liquid as it was pushed into my bloodstream.

I had a series of five injections over several weeks. After the last one, he said, 'You know they make this stuff out of monkeys?'

'Monkeys?'

'Rhesus monkeys. And chickens.'

'Wow.'

I was wondering which parts of the monkey and the chicken they used, but he must have taken my expression for pity.

'Better them than you,' he said.

I didn't think about him again. The bat bite was healing; it looked pink and raw, curdled. Several weeks later I went to a bar with a friend. When I walked in I saw him sitting on a barstool. He was watching a football game on the TV and eating from a bowl of free mixed nuts. I remember the way he ate those nuts, mechanically chomping through them, handful after handful, in a way that suggested neither enjoyment nor hunger; only process.

It wasn't until my friend had left and I'd paid my bill that I approached him.

'Not foaming at the mouth?' he said.

He was a little drunk.

'Not yet,' I said.

'Do you know how alcohol works?' he asked while I tried to get comfortable on the bar stool without letting my legs fall open.

'It removes your inhibitions,' I said, remembering something from a long-ago biology class.

He looked at me with a condescension so pure that it was more amusing than annoying, and I laughed.

'The molecules in ethanol,' he said, his own cheeks glowing pink, 'are small enough to pass into the gaps between brain cells. In the brain –' here he paused to suppress a belch – 'the alcohol binds to glutamate, a neurotransmitter which excites neurons. This is why alcohol makes a person slower to respond to stimuli.'

'Uh-huh,' I said. He had ignored my request for a cosmopolitan and ordered me a martini. I bit into the olive and instantly regretted it.

'Then there's gamma-aminobutyric acid,' he added, pronouncing the words carefully. 'It's not the ethanol itself that affects you, it's what it binds itself to.' He took my hand. 'That's what slows you down. That's what makes you susceptible.'

He was smiling at me, impressed with himself.

'I'm feeling pretty susceptible,' I said.

'Well then, let's get you home.'

What I remember most about that first encounter is the furiousness of it, Pete's teeth against my teeth, my clumsy hands on his buttons. That, and I remember lying there when his head vanished beneath the covers, wondering why his perfectly competent efforts were achieving so little. I remember thinking, Glutamate, glutamate, glutamate, and considering whether this might be the agent responsible.

When I woke up, I saw things more plainly. We were in a room that was nearly empty. I realised I had spent the night on an air mattress.

I turned over to see that Pete was awake, squinting at his phone.

'Is this an air mattress?'

If he flushed, his tan made it too hard to tell.

'It's a DreamWell,' he said. I could see the place between his pectorals where the skin puckered against the sternum and was again impressed by the effort it represented. 'They're the best on the market. It has plush-coil technology and an internal high-capacity pump.'

It turned out he'd been engaged until recently – the demise of this engagement some weeks earlier was behind his uncharacteristic visit to a bar. He told me her name was Megan Donaghue, but I never saw that name written down. Sometimes, even now, I will still while away twenty minutes googling the seemingly endless variants: Megan, Meghan, Meaghan, Donohue, Donaghue, Donoghue. At any rate, Megan/Meghan/Meaghan took everything, at Pete's insistence, including the bed. He wanted a fresh start, he said. He didn't want anything that reminded him of his past.

'I don't like the thought of it,' he told me one day when he was vacuuming the curtains. 'Just say you forget it's there – some photo or card or whatever – then *wham*, one day when you're not ready, there it is, staring you right in the face.' He shook his head.

I found out later that he'd scattered his parents' ashes, against their will, for the same reason. He was determined to be haunted by nothing.

From the outside, the second house looked like a Victorian cottage. Lacework, verandah, weatherboards. I'll admit it: I was charmed.

'An original,' Cilla said. '1860.'

I took in the lion's-head knocker, the bottle-green paint on the door. This was more like it, I thought. A country house that looked like a country house.

I thought it would be cosy inside, quaint. But standing in the hallway was like standing in a tunnel. It was dark, and narrow. There was a bright light coming from the back of the house, which was further away, much further, than I expected.

My eyes adjusted. I saw that the hallway was carpeted, and lined with waist-high pine panelling stained an oily yellow.

There were two bedrooms either side. I stepped into one of them. A wall hanging read *Live, laugh, love*, in a variety of life-affirming fonts. The quilt cover was patterned with gerberas. Even I could tell that the Victorian decor – the lamps, the bedframe, the standing mirror – were cheap reproductions.

The oily panelling that began in the hallway went all through the house – into the kitchen, the dining room, and through to the cavernous extension, where it spread into the third bedroom and the huge, sunken living room.

'This property has so much potential,' said Cilla in her mock-baby's voice.

I swallowed. The place made me feel like I was sinking. Like if I let my head slip below the level of that cheap yellow panelling, I might never resurface.

'I don't like the smell,' said Pete.

Cilla lifted her nose in the air. I saw her nostrils pulse and wondered whether she was flaring them on purpose.

'I don't smell anything,' she said.

I was glad to get outside.

I breathed deeply, took in the smell of cut grass. An image arose in my mind's eye: of my younger self, dodging and weaving on the lacrosse pitch. My long socks a blur, soaked through with

Saturday morning dew, the wet red so dark it was almost black. I'd loved those mornings. I loved walking onto the turf swinging my stick, feeling it slice the air. I even loved the stale dryness of my mouthguard, freed after days sitting unwashed in its box.

I took another deep breath and then another. A pang of something like grief hit me. I had been good at that game. Really good. I had to hang onto that thought. And if I'd never reached my potential, at least no-one could say it was my fault. No-one could say I hadn't worked hard. No-one could say I wasn't good enough.

We didn't even go into the third house. When Pete pulled up outside it – a tidy, priced-to-sell brick-veneer – and saw that the houses on either side were taller, newer, casting shadows on the dry, pale lawn, he just kept driving.

This was another of Pete's qualities that I found both attractive and repellent, the way he was willing to cut something off or out so mercilessly.

He told me once that he had had an ant farm as a child. He was enthralled by it, he said. He would stare, fixated, as the ants constructed intricate tunnels behind the glass, through the white sand.

But then the ants had started to die. The living ants dug a chamber where they would carry and dump their dead. It was depressing, Pete said. Each day the pile of dead grew and the number of live ants shrank.

In the end he picked up the thing and shook it hard enough to make all their tunnels collapse. He couldn't stand the thought of waiting until the last ant keeled over, with no-one to carry it to the mass grave. He said he couldn't remember ever feeling so relieved.

The final house was the one Pete most wanted to see. It was on a good street, a broad boulevard that rolled into the town centre. Cilla's hatchback slowed down at an amber light instead of accelerating, and Pete gnawed his bottom lip in annoyance.

By then the sun was lowering. It was the dirty end of the afternoon, when your collar is grainy and your lunch is sitting low in your stomach, and you begin to question whether you've done anything worthwhile with the day, with any of your days.

The urge to assess how well I'd used my time had only developed recently. When I used to play lacrosse I paid no attention to the time I'd spent, the percentage of my life that was gone. There was just school and training, and games on Saturday mornings. There was the steam of the showers. There were other girls' sweaty heads butting up against mine while we whispered tactics or shared our fury or our elation. I remember their small, strong fingers pressing into my shoulders. I remember rubbing lotion into my aching thighs on the bus home. I remember that I didn't have any doubts about my life and its purpose. But I can't remember what it was I thought about. Did I even have thoughts then? Or did I just unfurl like an animal every morning with no need to think, only move?

We arrived. Pete switched off the ignition. We watched Cilla try to get out of the car, catch the tiny heel of her shoe in the door and then have to remove the shoe to free herself. Pete did his yoga breathing, inhaling through one nostril and exhaling through the other. He did it with a steely focus on Cilla's little foot, her little shoe, her little car. He watched as she hopped to the kerb, still with a smile plastered onto her face.

He did five more rounds of pranayama while I listened to the breath enter and exit his body. At first I had been surprised by Pete's interest in yoga, his seriousness. I had no interest in something that would leave my hair smelling of feet and nag champa and remind me of the lingering instability of my knee. But Pete was oddly susceptible – not only to the practice of yoga, but to its trappings. Over time he'd amassed a collection of cheap buddha statues and positioned them throughout our apartment, avoiding the fatter, laughing buddhas in favour of the more svelte and serene.

Yoga, he said, focused his mind. It made him calmer, kinder. But still he looked at Cilla the way I'd seen him look at the homeless, at drunk people, at artists: anyone who wasn't being careful enough. Anyone who, in case of accident, would only have themselves to blame.

We got out of the car and stood looking at the final house. If you entered into a database every house that had been built anywhere in the past hundred and fifty years and programmed the computer to spit out the median house, the one right in the socket of average, this would be it. What can I say? Double-storey, single-fronted, white weatherboard. And clean. So clean the light bounced right off it without snagging on decoration or dust. A billboard advertising the house had been erected against the fence. Its headline read: *Sure to Impress.*

Pete rubbed his dry palms together, hard and fast like he was trying to start a fire.

'This is the one.' He turned and looked me right in the eyes. 'This is the one.'

Cilla came to stand by us. The wind blew strands of her hair into her lip gloss and she didn't try to extricate them.

'This place looks brand new,' I said.

Cilla gave a bright smile. 'It's a foreclosure,' she said.

She walked with jerky purpose up the smooth concrete paving to the front door.

Once inside, Pete scanned the place keenly.

'Three bedrooms,' Cilla said, consulting her notes. 'Master with ensuite and walk-ins. Fully insulated, with underfloor heating. The dishwasher and oven are as-new.'

We had walked into a white and grey open-plan living area with engineered floors. Everything was big, as though the place had been built for outsized people. The ceilings were high, the windows broad, the marble island in the kitchen long and exaggerated. Pete walked around touching nothing, respectful, as if he was in a church.

'Did I mention the gas log fire?' said Cilla, lisping in her baby voice.

She went to the wall and retrieved a remote control. She pressed a button and low blue flames sprung up to perform a pantomime of consuming the faux log at their centre.

We went to look outside, where Cilla showed us the covered entertaining area and the automated watering systems. We toured the downstairs bathroom, whose cabinets were lined with LED lights. Reverently, Pete flushed the toilet to test its pressure.

'There's also this,' Cilla said. She walked over to a wall. She retrieved another tiny remote, pressed a button, and the three of us stood in mute politeness as the blinds unrolled themselves slowly, smoothly, leaving the room in an artificial twilight. We stood in the intimate darkness for a moment. Then Cilla pressed another button and we watched the process reverse itself, the blind curling up and putting itself away.

'State-of-the-art,' Cilla said.

After the display ended we all kept staring at the blind for a moment, as though it might complete another trick.

Cilla turned to us. 'To the master bedroom?' she said.

She went to lead the way but Pete outpaced her. He took the steps two at a time. Soon he stood on the landing with his hands on his hips, wondering which of the closed rooms was the one he sought.

Cilla, her breathing heavy – I supposed she hadn't done any cardio since high school – turned right and walked the short corridor to a glossy white door. We followed.

'It's a generous room,' Cilla began, swinging the door open. 'South-facing windows, new pure wool carpets …'

Then it was as though we had crossed from one reality into another. Cilla's description was accurate, and there were white walls and heavy silver curtains to go with the plush, grey-beige carpet. The bed was huge, king-sized, dressed in what looked to be fresh white linen.

But in it, obviously naked, were a man and a woman. The man sat up. He was hairy, I remember that – I remember how thoroughly his body was furred, and that the hair on his head had volume as well as length. His glasses, his jewellery – rings, a chain – were on the bedside table beside him. The woman did her best to vanish under the covers but I could see her body beneath them, moving, could hear her limbs swishing against the sheets.

Perhaps some people would have screamed, or tried to explain. Weirdly, their first reaction was silence – the man just put out his hands, patting the air around him downwards, as though to calm us. I took in their belongings: not the shabby rucksacks or plastic bags that would indicate vagrants, but two large roller cases, with matching smaller overnight bags. I saw a handbag that would have been expensive. Overcoats. A laptop. Smartphones charging at the wall sockets.

Cilla didn't flush right away. In fact, her face went pale and waxy and she got this faraway look. I'd seen it when she was in my class – waiting to be picked for a team, trudging up to the softball plate. It was the look of someone still blankly waiting for a bus long after everyone else has realised it isn't coming.

The man kept patting the air in front of him. Finally, struggling, his voice breaking, he said, 'This house is not for sale. Okay? There's been a mistake. This is our house. *Our* house.'

Cilla remained rooted to the spot. Two paces away, so did I. It was Pete who walked up to the bed. He yanked the duvet off and threw it so far into the air it spun like flung dough. He ripped the sheet back, revealing the soft, hairy, warm bodies of the intruders.

The woman shrieked and went to cover herself, but Pete wasn't deterred.

'Get out,' he said. He clapped his hands, and I half expected the light to switch off.

When they didn't move, he clapped again and started shouting. 'Now! Out!'

The man, cowed, naked, said nothing more. Soon the couple were feeling about on the ground for their clothes, forgoing underwear in their haste to be covered. The woman, on her hands and knees, looked at me for a moment and then looked away. I saw her hand hover over a used condom, but she decided to leave it where it was.

Once they were dressed, Pete drove them out of the room as if they were sheep. Watching him use his height, his bulk, hearing the disgust in his voice, I felt that familiar mixture of attraction and distaste; distaste at his unkindness, but an undeniable attraction to the authority with which he evicted the couple from their property.

After they had left I slid the bedside drawer open, saw a hairbrush filled with the woman's hair, some pearl earrings which might have been real or might have been a good fake. I wasn't going to rub them against my teeth to check. I closed the drawer without disturbing anything.

Once the previous owners were outside, Pete stomped back up the stairs and into the master bedroom. He flung the window open. He went around the room gathering up the things they had touched – including the sheet, including the condom. For a terrible moment I was worried he would fling everything out onto the freshly trimmed front lawn, but he just stood there clutching it, furious.

Cilla swallowed. 'Thank you,' she said, gazing at Pete with a glassiness in her eyes. Her face was red now, a bright, flammable red. She was so grateful I could barely look. I thought she was going to cry.

Pete dropped everything on the floor. He put a hand to his face, pressing the heel of his palm into the bridge of his nose. Another calming technique; I'd seen it before.

Cilla pulled out her handkerchief, dabbed her mouth, then folded it up and kept folding until it could not be folded any smaller.

'Are you all right?' Pete said, his eyes still closed.

Cilla nodded. 'I'm fine.'

Pete's eyes opened. He lowered his hand. 'I wasn't asking you,' he said. He licked his lips.

Cilla's flush intensified.

'I'm fine,' I said. 'Pete? I'm fine.'

But now Pete had eyes only for Cilla.

'How did they get in here, anyway?'

Cilla shrank away from him, wilted away.

'Well?' Pete said. 'I asked you a question. This is someone's fault. Is it yours?'

Cilla mumbled something.

'What?' Pete put his hand to his ear and leaned forward. 'You'll have to speak up. I can't. Fucking. Hear. You.'

Cilla looked at me. It was a look I knew, a look that every gym teacher, every teacher, has seen a thousand times: a plea for mercy.

'Pete, come on, let's get out of here,' I said. I kept my voice flat, neutral. I didn't want either of them to think I'd taken the other's side.

'I'm sorry,' Cilla said on a puff of breath, giving that weird smile; only now it looked unhinged, panicked, the smile of a rabid dog. 'I'm sorry —'

'"Sorry, I'm sorry, so sorry,"' Pete said. He was imitating not only her voice, but her hunch, her gestures. 'Is that all you've got to say?'

Cilla looked down and crossed her arms, tight, like she was trying to tie herself into a knot.

Pete tucked his hands beneath his arms, assumed the wide stance he always favoured. He stared down at the top of Cilla's bent head. I turned away. If she was crying, I didn't want to know.

For a long moment nothing happened. Finally, Cilla turned and hurried from the room.

Pete looked at me and inclined his head in the direction she had taken.

'Pathetic,' he said.

Most of the drive home passed in silence. Pete applied his laser focus to the road, making precise turns, weaving in and out of the traffic to save time, even though there wasn't anywhere we needed to be.

'*Are* you okay?' he asked finally.

'Am *I* okay?'

'Not shaken up I mean.'

We rolled to a halt at a red light and he looked at me, serious.

'I can understand if you're upset.'

'I'm not upset,' I said. I remembered the couple's cowering bodies, their pale, sallow backs as they crawled on the floor.

'Are you sure?'

'Yes.'

'You can tell me.'

'I've seen dicks before, Pete.'

He flattened his mouth in distaste. 'That's not what I meant.'

I wondered whether he, too, was remembering how the man's penis looked when he rose from the bed; how it wavered half erect, uncertain of what it was doing; a grey-beige neutral shade not unlike the carpet.

'I felt sorry for her.'

'Don't,' he said, accelerating once the light went green. 'They probably overcapitalised.'

'No, not – I meant Cilla.'

Pete paused, genuinely surprised.

'Why?'

'She was so …'

'Weak?' Pete supplied. 'Scared?'

'I guess.'

'You don't have to pity her, Amy. Now I know why you hated her.'

'I never said I hated her.'

'Oh, you hated her. I can tell. And I can see why. That voice, that face – she's creepy. Makes my skin crawl.'

'She can't help it.'

'Like fuck she can't,' said Pete. 'That tongue – Christ – why the fuck's she never had that fixed?'

'What do you mean?'

He did an impression of Cilla's voice. '*Er ung*,' he said, quietly, childishly.

'Don't be cruel.'

'I'm not being cruel, I'm being accurate. She's tongue-tied.'

'Tongue-tied?'

He glanced at me, incredulous, before turning his attention back to the road. 'You didn't know?'

'Know what?' I said.

'Tongue-tied. You've never heard of it? Seriously?' He went into nurse mode. 'It's when the membrane holding the tongue to the floor of the mouth extends too far. The tongue has restricted movement. Don't tell me you didn't see it? The spittle? The dry lips? The little handkerchief?' He laughed in disbelief. 'You never knew?'

I felt a weird crawling feeling at the back of my skull.

'Of course I didn't fucking know.'

Pete shook his head, then shook it again. 'They used to do them at birth,' he said. 'Nurses would keep one fingernail long and sharp so they could cut the frenulum.' He swished his thumb through the air. 'Her parents should have had her fixed,' he said. 'But now she's an adult. Now she can fix it herself.'

I thought of all the times I'd spoken to Cilla, every time I'd seen her stumble and shrug her way through my class.

'Maybe she doesn't want it fixed,' I said.

Pete drove in silence for a few minutes, speeding in a straight line down the highway.

'I don't understand weird people. Why would anyone want to be weird?' he said.

He could have been talking about Cilla. Or the couple

crawling around on the carpet, grabbing up their things. He could have been talking about the hoser-downer, or the owners who installed the hideous pine panelling. The one person I knew he didn't mean was me.

I lied about the bat. To Pete, I mean. I'd lied when I said I'd been decisive, taken action; that this was the nature of my error. The truth was too embarrassing to tell.

I had first consulted the wisdom of the internet. Wait, was the advice. Bats have excellent echolocation; wait for it to find its own way out. Or failing that, wait for it to exhaust itself and fold up like a leathery cocoon somewhere. When it has, you can place a bucket over the bat and carry it outside.

So I sat down on my living-room floor, still careful with my bad knee after all those years. I waited for that bat to figure out how to leave my apartment. I waited and waited, watching it jerk around the light fitting, bumping against the ceiling, flailing, getting nowhere.

It was after it finally landed, after I'd slipped a bucket over it and slid the lid underneath, that it bit me. I held the bucket next to the open window and removed the lid, but there was no movement, no sound, and I was worried it was injured, maybe dead. I stuck my hand, stupid, stupid, into the dark recess of that bucket. It bit me because I sought it out, because I went to touch it gently with my fingertips.

That day I met Pete, when he asked me if I was a vampire, I started to wonder if it were possible that the bat had imparted something to me. Some new power or talent, some reserve of darkness or mystery on which to draw, something that would mark me as different, as changed.

In bed, while Pete operated himself above me like a piston, focused on a point on the wall, his toes braced against the foot of my bed, I would imagine drawing that new, essential thing up through myself, like casting a spell. But nothing ever happened. Maybe there was nothing dark in me, nothing strange, nothing special. Just the usual things: glutamate, amino acids, a normal frenulum, and one healed ligament that would always be at risk of rupturing again.

I thought about Cilla all that week. I found myself idly searching for her online, thinking it would be easy to find information about someone with such an unusual name. But all that came up was the profile at her father's real estate business: a black and white portrait of her looking washed out and stunned, a culprit, the way a possum looks when you shine a light in its eyes.

I waited until Pete was at his yoga class before I slipped out to the florist. Once there I stared and stared at the wall of flowers. Lilies, irises, orchids; it seemed like every flower had a free and mobile tongue and was intent on directing it towards me.

Finally I drew some white roses from their black plastic bucket. I chose green paper, a gold ribbon; in every choice I made I felt an aversion to pink, to purple, to red, to any pulpy, fleshy colours, anything you might see on the inside of a mouth.

I arranged for the delivery and bought a card.

'Here,' said the florist, handing me a pen.

I asked her to write it out for me. There was a chance, however small, that Cilla might know my handwriting.

I had considered every possible iteration of an apology: please accept my apology, sincerest, deepest, truly. Which one did I choose? I'm afraid I can't say. What I wrote is between me and Cilla, even if I did ask the florist to sign the card with Pete's name.

'Your name's Peter? How unusual,' the florist said, amused. She tucked the point of the envelope in.

'No. I'm not Peter.'

She gave me a knowing smile. 'You're not Priscilla, by any chance?'

I took the envelope from her, untucked its tip, licked along the glue and sealed it shut.

'No,' I said. 'I wish.'

Powerful Owl

The first part of Maya to wash up on shore was a foot. The cop they sent to break the news arrived on our doorstep with her cap under her arm. She knocked on the flyscreen, and the mesh shimmied under her knuckles.

When we opened the door, flies came in.

Her shoes stuck to the linoleum in the kitchen. She accepted a glass of soft drink and soon its neon green transferred to her tongue.

'You sure it's her?' said my mother.

'We're sure,' the cop said.

'What about Cameron? Where was he?' I asked.

Mum shot me a look.

The cop said they were not treating the circumstances as suspicious. Maya had been seen alone on the beach that night.

My mother didn't ask how Maya's body had come apart the way it did. So I asked instead.

'It's just the tide,' the cop said. 'It's natural.'

Other parts washed up over the weeks that followed. In the end Mum had to identify Maya from what they could assemble: a hand, a thigh, part of a torso with the spine hanging out.

Maya went into the furnace in a cardboard coffin.

My mother, once Maya was half a plastic container of ash, shook her straight back into the ocean she'd returned from.

'Serves her right,' she said.

Soon after that I decided to leave. My home town was starting to jangle my nerves. Watching the road become molten in the afternoon mirage. Wiping grit from my neck, licking salt from my upper lip. It had been years since I had noticed the dull pounding of the waves, but after Maya died it got to a point where I would lie awake unable to block out their constant, regular arrival, the wash and drag of it.

And we had other unending rhythms in that town: my mother lighting a fresh cigarette with a dying one, the race-caller's mounting panic coming over the car radio, the burr of static underneath. There were Saturday nights at the pub drinking vodka and raspberry until it came up in a pink rush against a wall, and boys who would holler their encouragement and kiss me anyway, as though this was a tender favour.

One Sunday, I put an ad on a website. I left it there a week. There was only one reply.

So this was who went to live in the hills, I thought.

How old was he? Forty-ish, I guessed, though he was thin enough and handsome enough to make his age seem like an advantage. His shirt was unironed. His lips might have been too broad, forming a rubbery oval like a clown's mouth, but he hid them with a beard. His bald spot wasn't alarming; it wouldn't have been larger than a dollar coin.

He gestured towards the child, who was sitting on a Turkish rug in a room lined with bookcases. White sunlight filtered in through glass doors that led to the garden.

'She's a good kid,' he said. 'I can't imagine she'll give you much trouble.'

I was relieved to hear him use a pronoun. The baby was dressed in sombre grey and white, and her short black hair provided me with no clues whatsoever. Her name, Lee, hadn't helped.

She wasn't so much playing as grabbing at the elegant objects that surrounded her.

'She keeps putting things in her mouth,' he said. 'You'll have to watch that.'

I told him that I would.

My references were as excellent as they were fabricated. My friends, all childless, had assured him I was conscientious, responsible, caring, patient. I was none of these things. But I was cheap.

His name was Marc. In one email, I had mistakenly addressed him as Mark. When he replied, he corrected me. *I don't mean to be a pedant*, he wrote, *but it makes a difference. A 'k' sounds harder. Like 'ark'.*

Personally, I couldn't hear the difference.

He showed me around the house. He walked me through an open-plan dining room and kitchen, the living room where the baby played. There was no television. The couches faced one another.

Upstairs was the child's room, and doors he didn't open: his bedroom, his office.

'No shoes in the house, by the way,' he said. 'Sorry. I should have mentioned it earlier.'

He looked at me while I leaned down and unlaced my sneakers. I'd thought them clean enough, but now could see the way grime had worked its way into the stitching.

When I was in my socks, he continued down the hallway to another closed door.

'This is your room,' he said, opening it.

It was like a room in a nun's cloister. Clean and white, with a child's wardrobe made of oak and a white single bed. A chest of three drawers sat beneath the window; on it was a tiny vase holding a single twig of eucalypt. Marc explained that the bathroom next door could be for my exclusive use. Mine and the baby's. He would confine himself to his ensuite.

'That's kind of you,' I said.

I stepped to the window and scanned the view: below was the garden, a damp mess of uneven grass and clumps of flourishing weeds, with tall ferns and bottlebrush around the perimeter. Beyond this were similar gardens behind similar houses. Beyond those, trees: at the end of Marc's street was the entrance to a national park.

'It's very nice,' I said, turning back to him. 'Your house.'

He walked into the room, pressed down lightly on the bed with a splayed hand.

'We like it.'

I could see the dimples left by his fingers in the quilt cover.

It occurred to me later that 'arc' was also spelled with a 'c'. Science was one of the subjects I hadn't failed. I remembered learning that an arc is a visible jolt of electricity: the jagging, blue-white path energy takes when it's finding the fastest way from one point to the next.

As for the wife, I never saw her. That's not completely true: I saw her all the time, smiling obligingly out of framed photographs. She was away on some kind of sabbatical – archaeological, I think, although I might have imagined that. They had a lot of artefacts around, which looked like they'd been dug up: limestone and soapstone, clay and flint.

Marc worked from home during the day except for Fridays, when he went to a university in the city to teach a seminar on torts. When he said this word I pictured cakes. I had worked in a bakery for a while. To me, tortes were dense Eastern European things that sat like stones in their boxes when I packed them up.

When I told him this, he smiled.

'A tort – my kind of tort – is a wrongdoing,' he said.

Still I pictured layers of dense wintery sweetness as foreign as snow.

'Say a man is driving a car and he veers off the road and over a cliff,' Marc said. The baby was in bed and we were drinking dandelion tea, a strong, swampy brew that stank like the chicory my great-grandmother drank. He was sitting on one couch. I was on the other.

'Say the man dies. Who's to blame? The driver? The car? The roads authority?'

'No-one,' I said. 'It's an accident.'

That made him laugh.

'You probably wouldn't like my class,' he said.

'What's the answer?'

'That depends. The average students would say the driver. The better students would think of a way to sue the manufacturer of the car, or whoever maintained the roads. The best students say things like "Well, for all we know, a bee flew into the car". They don't accept things at face value.'

I didn't know what to say. I was thinking of the pinch of a bee's sting when it lodges in your calf; the way rubber screeches when it's burned into a wild curve on the asphalt. I was thinking of that car smashing through the barrier and launching over the edge.

When Marc was working at home, my job was to maintain silence in the house. This meant keeping Lee quiet.

How long and slow the days became that spring. Often I spent entire afternoons speaking to no-one but the baby. At night I would lie still and hear the calls of nocturnal birds – trilling and knocking sounds, throaty sounds, calls that sounded like choking. And occasionally a *woo hoo … woo hoo … woo hoo* called long and loud over the night.

Marc had been correct about one thing. The baby didn't give me any trouble. She was good, quiet, a warm little weight that I picked up frequently, as much out of my own boredom as because she cried or reached for me.

But even good babies cry, and sometimes, though I jiggled her and sang to her and cooed and patted her back, she would wail and wail for a reason I couldn't discern.

Early on, at one of these times, Marc descended the stairs until he was standing on the bottom step, his toes in cashmere socks curling over its edge.

'Perhaps a walk?' he said.

'To where?'

There wasn't much where he lived. No shops in walking distance. No beach, no cafes.

He waved a hand irritably towards the trees. 'She likes it out there,' he said.

I went outside with the pram and pushed Lee to the end of the street. I could see the path that led into the park, where the trees shivered and made a hissing sound in the pollen-littered breeze. But I had no interest in approaching them.

I settled for walking up and down the street.

Eventually, the baby stopped crying.

I looked at her plump face, creaseless in sleep. It struck me that it was impossible to remember being a person to whom nothing terrible had happened. A person who wasn't conditioned to always be waiting for bad news; to always expect the worst.

I don't know what I was thinking when I wheeled Lee's pram to the middle of the road. There was no traffic. It's not as though I thought anything was coming. I just wheeled it out, left it there, walked back to the footpath and watched for a minute, or maybe two.

Lee didn't snap awake or even stir. She slept on, oblivious.

Maya and I were both flinchers.

Maya had liked Cameron's height. 'Six-six,' she said to me on the beach one day, when we were sinking one beer after another and letting the empties roll down the dunes. 'He makes me feel like a baby doll.'

The nun's room began to smell like me. The door was closed all day. Whenever I entered I could smell the scent of my sealed and sleeping body. I was surprised every time by its mustiness, by its potency.

One day I went into the nearest town and bought a candle to dissipate this odour. I paid for it out of the cash Marc gave me. That was our arrangement, cash in an envelope with nothing printed on it, once a week, usually a Friday. Whenever I smell cash on someone's hands – that sweaty, grubby smell – I still think of him.

The candle was sea salt and cedar. I bought it at one of the nicer shops. It was a Saturday, my day off. I had the night off too but there was nothing to do. I came home in the late afternoon to find Marc reading on the couch, one long thin leg slung over the other.

'Staying in tonight?'

'I thought I'd have a quiet one.'

I came back downstairs later in the evening. Lee had been put to bed. Marc was peeling a long white vegetable that I'd never seen before.

'It's a daikon,' he said when he saw me looking. 'Have you eaten?'

Usually we ate apart. I had a single shelf in his fridge, a modest arrangement of cans in his pantry. But that night I joined him for dinner. I wasn't sure what I'd be eating, but I knew there'd be no meat in it. I knew he was very keen on never harming the earth or the creatures that roamed it. And I knew this included creatures that I considered brainless – the mussels we prised from under the pier when I was young, the oysters we stole from farms when the tide went out.

He suggested we eat on the patio. I followed him outside.

He asked questions about me. Siblings? University? And what do you want to do eventually? I heard how narrow my life sounded as its components were paraded one by one in front of him. The unhemmed edges of my education. My one overseas trip, to Bali. My family working in their dull jobs: a deckhand, a dental nurse, a receptionist.

And then I heard it again, that low *woo hoo* coming at intervals, something between a voice and a woodwind instrument.

'What is that?' I said.

'An owl,' he said. 'The Powerful Owl, to be exact.'

We sat in silence for a moment, listening to it.

'Reminds me of one of the cases we discuss in class,' he said.

'Oh?'

'It's not a tort exactly, but the students like it. So – a man was accused of murdering his wife. She was found at the bottom of the staircase in a pool of blood. He had motive – they'd been arguing, and he stood to inherit a substantial sum from life insurance.

'Anyway, there were wounds on her head. They thought the husband had struck her with a fire poker or some such. This was in the US, by the way —'

'So they electrocuted him?'

Good, I thought, imagining the electricity lighting him up from the inside, those blue-white jolts finding their way.

'Not quite. See, the wife had hanks of her own hair in each hand. And there were little feathers too. And the shape of the wounds wasn't really consistent with a poker. Expert ornithologists said they looked like gashes caused by an owl's talons. Also this was in the mating season, when owls are at their most aggressive.'

'So … an owl did it?'

He shrugged, turning down his clown mouth in practised uncertainty. 'The theory is that an owl attacked her in the garden, and she then stumbled inside and collapsed on the stairs. But what do you think? That's what I ask my students. Who's responsible? Who's at fault? How many ways can you interpret the facts?'

Later I searched for information about owls. I learned that they did indeed swoop on humans, mistaking us for rats or mice. I learned that prey never saw or heard them coming, because their feathers were designed for silence: serrated on one edge, fringed on the other.

I learned that a half-kilogram owl could land on a mouse with the equivalent force of a ten-tonne truck.

After dinner, Marc rose to rinse the bowls and I followed.

He said, 'I suppose I should look in on her,' meaning the baby, and this is literally what he did. He leaned against the doorjamb, skinny arms folded across his chest, and looked.

'Is she okay?' I whispered.

'Fine,' he said.

'Well, goodnight I guess,' I said. I went to my room.

I have had too many soft knocks on my door to be surprised by soft knocks. I was glad that he did not invent some kind of pretext to come in. I put my phone down and he went to the lit candle. I thought he would blow it out. Instead, he pinched it between his thumb and forefinger. His belt buckle was level with my eyes.

My vision adjusted to the dark. Soon the light seemed white-blue in that room. I remember being surprised at how thick and impenetrable the bush of his pubic hair turned out to be. I remember tasting chicory on his breath.

Afterwards he stood and said, 'Would you mind getting up?'

'What?'

'Could you just get up please?'

He switched the light on. He put on his trousers. I put an arm over my breasts.

'Can I have my bra?'

He found it and passed it to me, dangling it from one outstretched finger.

I stood. What was on and in me started rolling downwards.

He started stripping the sheets from the bed.

'What are you doing?'

'This mattress is new,' he said. 'There's no protector.'

He pulled the sheets back and frowned at the colourless stain at the centre of the mattress. He left the room, and returned with the vinegar and baking soda they used to clean everything in that house, along with a child's tiny toothbrush. He scrubbed for a couple of minutes, then bundled the sheets in his arms.

'You should maybe sleep on the couch tonight,' he said.

I lay on that couch and heard the washing machine gurgle and churn. Beneath that I could hear things moving outside, through the darkness.

The next day I was woken by the sound of Marc dragging the mattress down the stairs.

'Would you mind?' he asked.

I helped him drag it into the garden.

'Sunlight is the best thing,' he said.

Upstairs Lee started crying.

'I'm going to take the baby out,' I said.

This time I followed the path into the trees. They didn't seem so wild once you were among them. The silver foil of chip packets glinted in the undergrowth. The bins were studded with wads of gum.

October could still be a cool month in those hills. It was warm in the sunlight, but as I followed the path, moving deeper into the shade of the trees, Lee must have sensed a drop in temperature, must have sensed the blocking of the light.

She started fussing. Then she took one of those huge inhales that meant she was going to scream. For some reason, though I had spent so many weeks listening to her screams, this time it was impossible to endure them. This presented itself to me as a fact: I couldn't tolerate them any longer. I needed to make them stop.

Please understand that the baby survived. I hardly hurt her. I didn't hit her or shake her.

Please understand that everyone left alone with a small child has wondered what they might get away with.

All I did was reach into the pram and pinch her tiny nose shut.

For how long?

Say two seconds?

Say five at the most.

There was sudden quiet. I watched the wrappers flapping in the breeze. I heard the sweep-rush and scrape of leaves flittering along the bitumen.

When I let go she looked at me like she was really looking at me, like she could recognise me.

'Let's go home,' I said.

The weather started to feel more like spring. The sun was brighter, harsher. I would sit by the window while Lee slept and watch my arms turn pink.

Soon her mother would return.

It took me too long to give up on the hope that Marc would come and visit me in the nun's room again. I only let go of the fantasy after I walked into the bathroom and saw him there with the little chrome bin balanced on the sink. There was something in his hand. He had an expression on his face like someone who had just broken in through the window.

I'd seen that look, the look of a guilty man caught unawares. Maya's apartment was empty by the time Cameron came by. I'd opened the door and walked in on him.

We'd stood staring at each other.

Cameron moved first. He began to inspect the place while I watched. He touched everything, knocking on walls and running his hand along the windowsills, checking his fingertips for dust.

'There's nothing here,' I finally said.

He came over to the doorway where I stood. He kept walking until he was only an inch or two away. I stepped back, crossed my arms.

'I was just looking,' he said. 'No harm in looking, is there?'

I stared hard at Marc's hand. I hadn't emptied the bin in a week. I had wrapped my tampons in toilet paper, tightly, like they were bodies that needed to be shrouded for burial. He hadn't asked about birth control, so I suppose he was relieved to unroll one of the little packages and see the evidence of his own safety.

I still remember his wide, startled eyes. I can see the little string, brown with old blood, trailing from his closed fist.

A few days before my time in the hills was due to end, I heard a loud noise upstairs. I looked up and so did the baby.

I ran up the stairs. When I got to the top I saw that Marc had reached the nun's room before I could.

I walked in behind him.

'Oh my god,' I said.

The candle I'd bought had exploded. There was broken glass, a spattering of white wax hardening on the floor and walls.

When I came closer I saw that it had left a black shadow in the shape of a small spiny cloud – a cartoonish *bang!* – on the drawers' smooth white surface.

Marc didn't say anything, just ran his fingers back and forth through his hair.

'I'll clean this up,' I said. 'I'll pay for any damage.'

'It's fine,' he said. 'Don't worry about it.'

He left the room and came back with a plastic bag, and together we picked up the shards of glass.

'You let it burn down too far,' he said.

'I'm so sorry.'

'It's fine.'

I let the silence stretch for a moment while we placed smaller and smaller shards of glass into the plastic bag. But then I couldn't stop myself. I said, 'I could have burned your house down.'

Our goodbyes were perfunctory. Marc paid me exactly what was owed and I patted Lee on the head, sure that she would have no recollection of me whatsoever.

I saw him working before I left. It was in the morning, before the sun was high and relentless. He had taken the chest of drawers into the garden and was sanding it, removing the white paint to show the raw timber underneath.

I peered down from my window, focusing all the energy of my gaze onto his bald spot, which gleamed with perspiration as he worked. It was the unlikely hot pink of a baby mouse. I was high enough to get a good, clear view of his thin body worrying at its task. I'm not sure whether he could sense me looking, feel the ferocity of my concentration. If he did see me, he gave no indication. For a moment this saddened me.

But then I thought that it was probably for the best. Yes, I thought. It would be best if he couldn't see me at all. It would be best if he never saw me again.

Arm's Length

They said: 'Keep that boy at arm's length.' But whose arm? The arm of an orangutan, a giant squid, a Tyrannosaurus rex? A spider's arm – and if so, which one of the eight should she measure? 'Your arm,' they said. So she took a saw and severed her arm at the shoulder. When they said: 'You still have your other arm,' she offered them the saw and said: 'Here. Go ahead.' Later, they planted the arms in the earth. No-one knew they grew roots, which reached for one another underground.

Harbour

'Listen to this, Nina,' said Tilly. 'The Common Death Adder. *Acanthophis antarcticus*. Has the longest fangs of any snake in the country. Highly venomous, producing a neurotoxin that can paralyse and kill a human in six hours.'

'Stop it, Tilly.'

She'd bought a book called *What Snake Am I?* and had been reading out excerpts for the entire journey. We needed books where we were going; no devices were allowed. The book showed, in loving glossy detail, the snakes we might encounter: Taipan, Black Headed Python, King Brown. There were white-crowned and golden-crowned snakes, snakes that were egg-laying and snakes that were live-bearing, snakes that killed by poison and snakes that held you a little tighter each time you breathed, until you couldn't breathe at all. *If you find a pile of hatched eggs in your garden*, the book said, *look out*.

Tilly knew I was terrified of snakes.

'Look – Olive Python swallowing a wallaby. The python will feed on a wallaby's decomposing carcass for three months.'

'Enough.'

Tilly placed a hand on my knee. 'Pains?'

'Flying always makes it worse.'

'You should take something for it.'

'I don't have anything. Dr Bellavit says it's not allowed.'

'I know,' said Tilly. 'But I thought – well, just in case there's an emergency.'

She unzipped her handbag, then unzipped one of its secret compartments. Inside was a blister pack of painkillers, hospital-strength, some kind of morphine. We had a supplier. The pills were out of date but usually this meant nothing. I took two. I knew not to take any more. Once I took six and slept for twenty-two hours. Tilly had to keep checking my pulse. If it had slowed too much, she said, she would have taken me to emergency. But then there might have been trouble.

We never liked dealing with our supplier. He seemed greasy. The pores around his wide nose gaped, and he bounced his leg incessantly when he sat, his belly spreading over the tops of his thighs.

Unfortunately, dealing with him was necessary. No doctor would give us the prescriptions we needed, even though we told them again and again how unwell we were. We both had digestive disorders. There was pain, sometimes dull, sometimes acute; there was an unpleasant fullness, where our guts felt solid as brick and nothing moved. Often we'd examine one another in the mornings and see how our gums and tongues lacked colour, how the blood vessels were swollen in our eyes. There were days when we could hardly leave our beds. We'd leave the curtains drawn and run the same Google searches we'd been running for years:

bad digestion new therapies
digestive issues solution

chronic pain alternative practitioners
digestive health and wellbeing retreats

It was on one such day that I found Dr Bellavit.

'Look at this,' I said. '*Harbour: A Place for Healing.* It's up north. On an island.'

'I hate the tropics.'

'Says she's cured a man of cancer.'

'They all say that.'

'Rheumatoid arthritis. Diabetes. This guy was cured of gout. Dr Bellavit is a miracle worker, he says. And it's all natural; it's based on a diet.'

This got Tilly's attention. 'How long would we stay for?'

'It doesn't say.'

The images showed a coconut grove, tall palms bending in a field of vivid grass, surrounded by a luxuriant tangle of rainforest. A colonial-era house – renovated, three storeys, and glaringly white – stood in the middle. The grove gave way to a white sand beach. I could imagine us there, Tilly and me, lying silent in the sun, sand sloughing off our dead skin, salt thickening our hair. We would float in the water while longer, slimmer versions of our bodies appeared as shadows along the seabed.

I emailed an enquiry, and in return was posted two application forms and a copy of Dr Bellavit's book: *The Expulsion Cure.*

'Expulsion?' Tilly was dubious. She was still trying our last diet, which involved eating 90 per cent fermented foods. All she ate was sauerkraut and tempeh, kimchi and pickles. She drank litres of kombucha. A monstrous scoby floated in a jar in our fridge, slick and floppy and yellow like a layer of fat. I had abandoned the fermented diet when I realised how bad I smelled: perpetually gassy, like a compost heap.

'We're turning into mummies,' I'd said.

'But don't you feel better?'

I took my belly in both hands, squeezed it.

'Not yet,' I said. 'Do you?'

'I've lost three kilos.'

The Expulsion Cure, explained Dr Bellavit in her introduction, was based on one simple idea: we are all poisoning ourselves. Modern life, with its nanoparticles and parabens, its additives and expedients, is killing us. We ingest things that the human body cannot process. We hold onto them and it makes us sick. And the digestive system is particularly susceptible to such attacks.

'So what does she mean by expulsion?' Tilly asked, curled on the couch with a hot water bottle. She sipped her kombucha. 'Is it like getting expelled from school?'

'Same principle.' I was drinking a tisane made from stinging nettles. It was bitter, but I liked to think of it scrubbing my insides like drain cleaner, removing the scaly deposits, leaving things shiny. 'You identify the undesirables and you throw them out.'

'Where do they go?' she asked.

'They vanish,' I said.

After the flight, we hired a driver to take us out of town to the ferry terminal. As far as we knew, there were no other residents on the island besides those at Dr Bellavit's retreat. The ferry's windows were filmed with grease, and there were seams of grime worked into the cracks in the plastic seats.

As we boarded, the ferry driver said, 'Staying with Dr Bellavit?'

'Of course,' I said.

The man spat into the water. He seemed fascinated by the small foamy spot of it floating away.

'It's just – you don't look sick.'

He raised his gaze back to us. His neck and chest were a deep, uniform pink-red. I was aware of how the heat made my clothes cling, of the salt in my mouth from where I'd licked sweat from my top lip.

'We are sick,' Tilly said.

The driver raised his hands as if in surrender.

He wasn't the first person to suggest we weren't really sick. We'd had doctors tell us as much. I was once asked by a psychiatrist if I understood the concept of secondary gain. I nodded enough to get prescriptions for Xanax and Zoloft, listening to the mucus in his nostrils – he was perpetually sniffing – vibrate as he talked.

Aunt Caroline doesn't believe us either. She's the one who took care of us after our father died. Her body looks like a fridge on top of two twigs. She used to accuse us of inventing our symptoms as an excuse not to study or to work.

'The only thing making the two of you sick,' she'd say, 'is each other.'

When we alighted from the ferry, the driver hauled our bags ashore. He gave me his card – a flimsy thing, homemade, with his name and phone number printed on it.

'Call me,' he said, 'if you decide you've had enough.'

Tilly plucked the card from my hand and tried to throw it away. It spun madly in the breeze and blew back towards us, before skittering away along the beach.

The ferry man didn't move until we were up the beach and swallowed by the grove. I saw our two sets of footprints winding around each other, Tilly's and mine, and tried to work out whose was whose.

'Doesn't look like the picture,' Tilly said.

'It's the wet season.'

But she was right. The colours were murkier. Piles of debris rotted languorously where the grove stopped and became forest. There was the smell of decomposition, too; sweet and sulphuric.

I took a step forward and snapped a stick in two. A foot from Tilly something slithered away, too quickly to see what it was. We exchanged a look.

'Could have been anything,' I said.

We stopped for a moment to admire the coconut trees. There were so many. Some were so close to the house they could almost touch it. The house itself both looked like the pictures and didn't. It was the same stately white weatherboard place with iron lacework and a broad verandah. But it looked scruffy, grimy, like it had just woken up after a bad night.

A coconut fell and landed with a thud.

'Strange-looking things, aren't they?' said Tilly, walking over to pick it up. 'It's like they have faces.'

I saw what she meant. It did seem to have two eyes and an open mouth; an animal face, covered in hair.

Tilly held the coconut in front of her own face. 'Boo!' she said.

'Hush,' I said. There was a figure in the doorway.

The first thing Dr Bellavit did when we entered the house was take each of us into her arms and squeeze. To me, she whispered, 'You're going to be okay.'

Dr Bellavit was more solid than I was expecting. Short, intensely tanned, muscular; the balls of her calves were high and prominent, her breasts a single floating apron beneath a white dress. Her eyes were bright against the baked brown of her skin.

She smelled of coconuts and sweat. There was no deodorant at Harbour, no toothpaste, no shampoo. These, we learned, were some of the rules. Once we had left our bags in the hallway, to be carried upstairs by the silent, white-clad orderlies who roamed the house, Dr Bellavit told us the rest. All of our valuables were to be locked in a safe in her office. There were to be no devices in the house, no medicines, no unauthorised food. No books except for *The Expulsion Cure*; Tilly's snake book and my paperbacks were confiscated. No talking unless it was with her. No electric lights – at Harbour, everyone lived by the sun. And no shoes.

'No shoes?' said Tilly.

'You won't need them.'

Our shoes went into the safe with everything else.

We were given a brief tour of the dining room, common area and kitchen, all of them clean and spartan, with white walls, dark furniture made from coconut wood, and coir mats on the floor. Then we were led up the winding wooden staircase to our rooms. They were next to one another. I wondered, when I saw mine, whether Tilly's was the same: almost bare, with an inch-thin mattress on wooden slats, a hard pillow, an unvarnished table, a bowl with a pitcher sitting in it. The window had no curtain. I had a view of the incinerator into which the orderlies dumped Harbour's rubbish. It was always hungry, always belching black smoke.

Each room had an ensuite and in mine I saw a curious thing. Above the bath there was a kind of seat. It was bolted in but had a hole in the middle. It must be for invalids, I thought.

I met Tilly back on the landing, where Dr Bellavit waited for us.

'Now,' Dr Bellavit said, smiling. 'Do you have any questions for me?'

'Yes,' said Tilly. 'Are there death adders here?'

'Excuse me?'

'Death adders. The snakes?'

'Oh – yes. Horrid things. We used to see them. But then the toads came,' she said. 'And that was that.'

The next morning Dr Bellavit called me in for a private interview.

'You must tell me everything,' she said, settling in her coconut-wood chair. 'There is no shame here. This is not a house of judgement. You must tell me all the details, and leave nothing out.'

A fan swung loosely overhead.

I crossed my ankles. 'Everything?'

She said the treatment wouldn't work if I kept secrets. She said that she would touch me, and know; that the secrets would ball my muscles into knots, swell my joints. She said maybe the things I refused to tell were part of my sickness. A sick mind, she said, will manifest in the body.

She took a notepad and a pen and told me to begin at the beginning.

Dr Bellavit's questions were frank. How much did I expel? And how often? And what is the colour? The texture? Is there pain? And how would you describe that pain – is it an ache, a stabbing, a burning? Is it dull or exquisite? Is there ever blood? How much? When you eat something – poppy seeds, say, or the skin on a plum – how long does it take to reappear?

I gave my answers and Dr Bellavit wrote them down, nodding, taking her time.

She said, 'I cannot say I am surprised. I can tell by looking in your face – the whites of your eyes look off. And if you could open your mouth – ah yes, there's a white fur on your tongue. I can see the vessels in your temples. Your gums are too pink. All the signs are there.'

'Of what?' I asked, though I knew what she would say.

'Toxicity,' she said.

She told me I had been poisoning myself. There was too much in my body. Too much bad food, bad air, atmospheric poison, emotional distress, too much unspent energy. I was blocked.

'These things build up, turn into toxic substances – your blood becomes acidic. Expulsion is what you need.'

I didn't say anything at first. I was imagining my blood as something quick and toxic, like mercury.

Dr Bellavit was staring straight into my eyes.

'It does worry you, doesn't it?' she said. 'All the things you're carrying?'

I said yes. I said that I could feel the weight of things inside me. I said it felt like concrete had been poured into my stomach, my heart chambers, my ribcage, and left to set. I began to cry – to really cry, hot tears wetting my cheeks and making dark spots on my shirt.

'Good girl,' said Dr Bellavit. She rose from the desk and came around to where I was sitting, pulling my head into the softness of her belly.

'Hush, Thomasina. It's quite all right. We'll get it all out, don't you worry. You'll be amazed by what will come out!'

The first phase of the expulsion cure lasted one week.

We had been warned before arriving that the first week was when most people failed. This was the time when the body was purged of the initial poisons circulating in the bloodstream, prior to the work of purification, of resetting the appetite.

For that week, all I was allowed to ingest was the cloudy water from a coconut. A strange taste, not sweet and not bitter; not much of anything. I was given two glasses of it per day: one in the morning and one in the late afternoon. I'd file into the dining room with a few other residents, all of us silent in the loose white linen clothes Dr Bellavit provided: plain shifts like nightdresses, for both women and men. I looked for Tilly, but she was never there at the same time I was.

When the hunger began, I read from Dr Bellavit's book. *You will experience what feels like hunger. This sensation may be unpleasant, even uncomfortable. Yet it is imperative that you do not accede to your baser instincts. You must expel their force from your body to let the healing begin.*

I did what she suggested and undertook positive visualisation exercises, imagining myself pulling in clean air and expelling poison with each breath.

But it didn't take long for my mouth to dry out and my stomach to grow hollow. I began to see everything in terms of what was wet and what was dry, what was edible and what was not. These boundaries grew less and less distinct. On the evening of the fifth day, I looked at the damp towel in my bathroom and wondered whether it would be cheating to twist its contents into my mouth. When I saw Dr Bellavit, I noticed how much her head, with its broad forehead and tiny, receding chin, resembled an egg. I could not focus on what she was saying for thinking about tapping a spoon against it, and salting the rich yellow yolk within.

'This is normal,' said the egg, nodding deliciously at me. 'This is good.'

By then I knew what the strange chair in the bathroom was for. It had become part of the structure of my days.

In the morning there was the white juice of the coconut, followed by cleansing. When Dr Bellavit first appeared in my room carrying a hose and a bag, I said, 'What's that?'

She locked the door.

It was to scrub away the toxins, she explained. They had adhered to the walls of my bowel; they were corroding me like rust. 'Our line of attack must be direct,' she said.

And every afternoon, I received a massage. 'The poison is in the fibres of your muscles,' Dr Bellavit said. 'It lives in the fascia, encasing them; it is all through your organs.'

I would lie on my bed and clamp my eyes shut as her hands came down on my back in fists. Each time they connected she chanted, 'Expel, expel, expel.'

Afterwards she held me as though I were a child, and let me cry. Often she didn't leave the room until I was asleep.

Later, people asked me whether I knew others who'd been at Harbour. Did you see my brother, did you see my wife? Yes, I said. I saw others at Harbour. I was forbidden from speaking to them. I saw them shuffling down the passageways, barefoot in their linen shifts, their mouths drawn thin, their eyes huge. And I heard them, day and night. I heard the wailing and the sobbing coming from their rooms.

They all looked so much older than us. So much worse. At the beginning I pitied them.

—

Dr Bellavit wanted to know what it was I was holding onto, emotionally.

We talked about my father and mother, little more than blurred shapes to me by then – a bark of laughter, a bracelet slipping down a wrist, the rustle and crack as the morning's newspaper was shaken out. We talked about Aunt Caroline: her blue eyeliner and hair gel, the word she taught me when I was seventeen: *malingerer.*

'You are what, Thomasina, twenty-eight years of age?'

'Twenty-nine.'

'And you have never known other types of torment? Those that might be inflicted by a boyfriend, say? A paramour?'

She smiled encouragingly.

'No,' I said, though even as I said it I saw Gordon's face, his narrow hips swaying as he danced in our living room, his fork ensuring the peas and corn were separate on his plate.

'Thomasina,' Dr Bellavit said, 'I understand your reluctance. I know that you are close with your half-sister.'

I sat up at this. It was true that Tilly and I were half-sisters. She had her mother's fair skin and honey-flecked eyes, the kind of hair that turns blonde in the sun. I looked nothing like her. My father always said: *you are as dark as a pirate*. And it was my mother's illness I had inherited, though she never had a diagnosis for it. She never sought treatment. She would only say she was *delicate*, and vanish discreetly to the powder room for hours on end. I never asked about the source of Tilly's illness. We never spoke of our different mothers. It was the one thing that, even in our worst arguments, stayed unsaid, hovering in the air.

But I hadn't mentioned this to Dr Bellavit. Tilly must have told her.

Dr Bellavit gave me a stern look. 'You must understand that you are here as an individual. Not as half of a pair. This is your time.'

She reached across the desk, took my hand. 'And your path to wellness will be unique. Do you see?'

She was smiling at me again. I didn't want to fail her test. My guts slithered in a spasm of pain. I nodded.

'Good girl,' she said, and clicked her pen.

In the evenings, we were allowed to walk to the beach. This is where Tilly and I found one another and broke the no-talking rule.

The island was never quiet. It wasn't just the swishing of palms, the woody scrape of their tips against the windows of the house. It was birds screeching in the mornings, frogs bleating in the evenings. And all through the days and nights the electric buzz of insects was in the air and the grass. They would cease when you stepped near, begin again when you were far enough away.

One evening, about two weeks after we'd arrived, Tilly said, 'I was allowed rice today.'

We were sitting on the beach and the wind was blowing. The sand stung our bare limbs.

'Rice?' Even the word was delicious. I thought of the hot grains, the starch they would leak, of chewing them into a gluey mess.

'Because of my progress,' Tilly said. 'You're still on water?'

'Water, coconut oil, sometimes an apple. And coconut paste.'

'I hate that paste.'

'I can't believe she gave you rice.'

'My toxicity is lessening. She thinks I can handle it.'

My gut clamped. Tilly covered her feet with sand.

'Sorry,' she said. 'I shouldn't have told you.'

But I could tell how pleased she was. I could hear it in her voice. Like when she passed a piano exam I hadn't taken, or was accepted into the accelerated English class at school.

Gordon hadn't believed we were sisters. Not at first. 'She looks nothing like you,' he'd said. It was the first night I'd brought him home and we were lying in bed, facing one another in the darkness. Tilly was only inches away, on the other side of the wall. But in the dark, that wall was invisible.

In the beginning, when Dr Bellavit explained the entire process to us, she said, 'I'm telling you this now, before the toxins within you feel threatened and begin to react. These toxins are like any enemy. As you wear them down, they become more desperate, more violent; you must have the fortitude of spirit to see them out. Do you understand?'

I thought of this as the weeks passed at Harbour. Dr Bellavit was giving me extra cleanses, extra massages; some days there would be a small, dry square of bony white fish, but on others I was back to only coconut water.

We had been warned that the 'final stage' would affect each of us differently. Some people were unable to sleep. Others had terrible spasms. Some entered a state of euphoria; sadly, I wasn't one of them. For me, it was my legs. They began to fail. They would shudder as I walked; I couldn't go downstairs without leaning on the banister, the muscles in my arms and chest quivering.

One night I awoke and the cramps in my legs were surpassed by the urgency of my hunger. I could think clearly. There was a voice in my head – I wondered, briefly, if it was God's voice – telling me to go downstairs.

When Dr Bellavit caught me, I was sitting in the kitchen. Most of the cupboards were locked but I'd found an open jar of coconut oil in the refrigerator. I hadn't bothered to search for a spoon. I was eating it with my hands, rubbing my wrist raw trying to dig further and further into the semi-solid white wax.

She didn't say anything. She just watched as I kept eating, twining my tongue around my fingers, helpless as an animal.

Dr Bellavit believed in punishments for breaking the rules.

'Please understand,' she said sadly, 'that I'm not punishing you. I am punishing the toxic things inside you.'

She didn't tell me how long I'd have to stay outside. In the morning I was sent out without shoes, or a hat or a blanket. All the colours seemed violent. The hissing of the trees and the wash of the tide were outrageously loud. I stayed out of the sun and kept my eyes shut. I was so still that the island's creatures stopped trying to avoid me. By evening, tiny lizards were darting over my hands.

Almost asleep, I was startled by the wet flop of a toad landing on my face. I sat up. The toad fell to the sand, the grotesque balloon of its throat contracting and expanding.

Eat it, the voice said to me. I knew, distantly, vacantly, that cane toads could kill me, as they had killed the adders. But still I wanted nothing more than to swallow it whole.

I reached for the toad. But there was no muscle behind the effort. The thing groped away through the long grass.

You snake. I'd said that to Tilly, years ago, when I found out what she'd done. I'd called her other things, too, but that name seemed particularly apt. She had waited and chosen her moment. She'd only needed to strike once.

After I was allowed back inside, I was taken straight to Dr Bellavit's office.

'I must discuss something serious with you, Thomasina,' she said. Her eyes were round like scallops, and I could smell meat in her sweat. She took my hand.

'Yes?' I said. My voice sounded like it was coming from somewhere else, as though another person were speaking.

'Matilda told me about her mother,' Dr Bellavit continued. 'She says that her mother suffered with her digestion all her life. There was pain, bloating, elimination issues. She was …' She paused, consulting her notes. '… delicate. Matilda tells me that it was only after she conveyed this to you that you started to complain of similar symptoms.'

'No,' I said. I shook my head, which made me dizzy.

I wanted to explain but couldn't form the thoughts. The things I needed to say felt far away. I looked down. My breasts were almost gone; I could feel my bones ache where the chair pressed in too hard.

'I think we need to consider the possibility,' Dr Bellavit continued, softly, 'that the poisons which affect you originate in the mind.'

I licked my dry lips. And then I blurted it out. 'She has medicine,' I said.

Dr Bellavit withdrew her hand. 'What?'

It was a gamble. I didn't know if Tilly had anything hidden in her room. But I knew her the way a sister knows her sister. I knew where she used to keep things when we were younger: a roll of money in her retainer case, a bag of pills in the spine of a book.

And my instincts were correct. I lay on my thin mattress and stared at the ceiling while the orderlies searched her room under Dr Bellavit's supervision.

While I lay there, an incident surfaced in my memory. I must have been ten, eleven years old. My father was drunk. He lurched into the living room, where I was sitting on the sofa watching television. Tilly was curled up next to me, asleep. My father said, 'You're not mine, you can't be. Look at you.' He pointed at Tilly. 'That one's mine,' he said.

From my window I saw Dr Bellavit toss what she'd found into the incinerator. She didn't turn back to the house immediately. She stood and watched it burn.

That evening Dr Bellavit arrived at my door with a glass of coconut water, and – my heart soared to see it – a small dome of rice in a white bowl.

This is where time breaks into pieces. I know that I slept and drank coconut water and saw Dr Bellavit, who would whisper encouraging words into my ear. 'They've stopped, haven't they, the pains?' she would ask. In some ways she was right. I lived in a small room inside myself, had abandoned the rest. 'You are almost through. It's almost over,' Dr Bellavit would say, and I'd put my head in her lap and sleep.

Only one memory remains distinct. It was night. There was a noise outside my door.

I thought I called, 'Hello?', but the distance between what I asked my body to do and what it did had grown so great I could no longer be sure. I opened my eyes, and saw them pass: two orderlies, and between them a stretcher whose occupant was covered by a sheet. Dr Bellavit passed behind, and I saw her turn her head and look at me through the open door. She had the face of a coconut: dark, surprised eyes and an open mouth. I was sure she knew my eyes were open. I was sure I heard her say, *'Boo!'*

I don't remember leaving Harbour. I don't remember much until one morning, weeks later, when my eyes opened with a snap and my thoughts were clear again. There was an IV in my arm and Aunt Caroline sat by the bed.

'Thomasina?'

'Where's Tilly?' My voice sounded strange – hoarse, foreign. Old.

'We'll talk later,' Aunt Caroline said. Her blue eyeliner looked electric, wet with tears.

Later, we learned that Dr Bellavit would place bodies in the incinerator. They found forms that I'd signed, forms that Tilly had signed, giving Dr Bellavit our inheritance, our house, our power of attorney. You won't get the body back, the police said. So we did the next best thing and asked to be sent the ashes from the incinerator. Tilly would like this, I thought. Being so small, so light, that she could slip into a narrow white-and-gold urn.

It was placed at the centre of Aunt Caroline's mantelpiece. We never discussed the possibility that the ashes might be someone else, or might be no-one – only Harbour's other refuse: burned-up coconut shells, grass clippings, swept leaves, household rubbish.

But there must be something of her in there, I thought. So one day, when I was alone in the house, I hobbled down the stairs – it still hurt to walk – and I took the urn down. My heart fluttered as I removed the stopper. I licked my fingertip and dipped it in.

I was surprised at the feel of the ashes. I had imagined them to be coarse, granular, but they were soft as flour, silken to the touch.

I tasted them again, and then a third time, before returning the stopper and putting the urn back in its place. I wondered how long it would take to digest Tilly, how long the specks of her body could sustain me. I wondered how long it would be before my body absorbed all traces of her – how long I'd have to wait to be sure she was really gone.

Monstera

It always seemed tragic to me that Ian was so much shorter than his daughters. He must have seen it coming – he must have seen their tibias and femurs getting longer and longer, seen their heads rising up to his shoulder and past it, past his chin, past his ears. By the time they were in high school, they could look down on the part in his hair. Whether or not this bothered him was hard to tell. Perhaps he was used to being a small man by then.

Of course, I was taller than Ian, too, but this didn't seem such a personal affront. I was an incidental, floating presence; a friend of his eldest daughter, Joanna. Whenever I went to the Mortons' house as a child he would ask a couple of questions about school and then say, 'Well, I'll leave you to it,' as though Joanna and I were about to conduct business more important than venturing outside to pull buds off the neighbour's camellia trees.

This was why I was surprised when he called me. We had no rapport, at least not one I knew about.

'Susie?'

'Yes?'

'Ian Morton.'

A pause.

'Jo tells me you're looking for work.'

Joanna was about to embark on a semester-long exchange. But right now, before it began, she was on a skiing holiday Ian had paid for. It was somewhere whose name was at once familiar and foreign to me: St Moritz, Aspen, Courchevel. In my mind these were all the one place, twinkling and brittle beneath the pale gaze of the sun.

'I guess so,' I said. I had recently quit my job at a market-research call centre because every night they had me working on a survey where I was supposed to find women aged over thirty-five to answer twenty minutes of questions about incontinence. 'And when you experience urine loss,' I'd say, 'do you lose a teaspoon? A tablespoon? Or the whole bladder?'

'I might have an opportunity for you,' Ian said. 'If you're interested.'

'Okay.'

'You don't sound interested,' he said. There was a breathy little laugh, and I had the sense I was on thin ice. I pictured Ian Morton as I'd last seen him: his too-big shirt tucked into his too-big jeans, his belt on the very last hole, its tail curling halfway around his waist. Supportive sneakers. Longish hair, round glasses. An elfish, ill-at-ease figure.

'Sorry,' I said. 'No, I am interested. Really.'

He cleared his throat. 'As you know, Joanna won't be back for several months. I thought you might fill in for her. As my dining companion.'

This, I realise, requires some explanation. Ian's wealth came from his company, which supplied mystery shoppers and mystery diners to businesses hoping to gather intelligence on their staff.

I remember Joanna telling me that the people who worked for him – the shoppers, the diners – were willing to work for almost nothing. A free sandwich. A pair of socks. A cinema ticket. This was the genius of his enterprise.

'They don't get paid?' I'd asked.

'They take what they can get,' Joanna said.

But there were some jobs Ian liked to do himself. Primarily, they were in the category he called Platinum Dining.

'So,' said Ian. 'Do you have any nice dresses?'

'I think so,' I said, looking at the bare rack where my clothes should have hung, and then to my bed, where they'd migrated, gradually, to form a shabby heap on its unoccupied side.

'I mean, appropriate,' Ian said, a smile in his voice. 'Nothing too tight or short. Nothing – what's the word? – *sheer.*'

'Whatever you want,' I said.

On the day of our first dinner Ian phoned me.

'Susie,' he said, 'I wonder if you might do me a favour.'

'Sure.'

'Would you be able to drive tonight?'

I was relieved that I had a ready answer. 'I would – but I don't have a car.' I barely had a bus ticket.

'We can take my car,' he said. He moved some sputum up from his throat. 'You remember our address?'

How many times as a teenager, waxy headphones plugged into my ears, had I taken the two separate buses to arrive at Joanna's place? How many afternoons had I whiled away in that sprawling house, or waist-deep in the swimming pool in the backyard?

Of course I remembered.

As soon as Ian answered the door, I could tell something was wrong.

'Come in,' he said. I followed him down the hallway. He was ginger on his feet, limping, hoisting his elbows with each step as though he could lift the pain out of his body.

'Are you okay?' I asked. 'We can cancel.'

'I'm fine. But you'll have to bear with me.'

I looked around. I hadn't been to the house since Joanna had moved out to live in a college on campus. But the place hadn't changed. The piano was still there in the living room, along with the leather lounge suite and the family photos on the wall: all four Mortons against a cloudy blue background.

I had chosen to wear what I thought was the most appropriate of my dresses – navy wool, boat-necked, knee-length, a garment that I thought was beyond reproach. But Ian looked it over with a cool expression.

He reached out and pinched a loose thread between his fingers, twisted it, then let it go.

'Don't try too hard,' he said.

Ian was wearing a grey sports jacket that was too big, but then most men's clothes were too big on him. He wore the same vaguely therapeutic-looking sneakers, tan slacks, a check shirt. I took a tissue out of my bag and blotted off some of my lipstick.

I didn't think it polite to ask what was wrong with Ian, so I crossed the open-plan space to the kitchen and drank a glass of water while he limped around the house, getting ready.

I didn't want the water so much as I wanted to see the kitchen, run the tap, remember the place. The glasses were in the same cupboard. And they were the same glasses: heavy-bottomed, square, with stickers that informed the drinker they were made in Czechoslovakia.

I looked out the floor-to-ceiling living room window and was amused to see a relic of my childhood that I'd forgotten: the huge, twisted monstera plant that lived in the Mortons' backyard.

Ian entered the room and saw me looking. 'Hideous, isn't it?' he said. 'The former Mrs Morton managed to kill every other plant we owned. But this one seems to thrive on neglect.'

I looked away when he mentioned his ex-wife. The Mortons had divorced while Joanna and I were in our first year at university. Joanna hadn't seemed too perturbed by it. 'I just don't get it, that's all,' she'd said. 'I mean, why get divorced when you're old? What's the point?'

She also told me that her father had managed to win himself a favourable settlement by having her mother followed by a private investigator for a month. It was how he'd kept the house. I always hoped she'd tell me what the investigator found, but she never did. She just said that she'd found the photos among Ian's things. 'There were so many of them,' she said. 'And they were so close up.'

I set my glass down on the sink.

'Ready?' I said.

The car was a heavy, low-slung convertible. To get into it, Ian gripped the roof and hauled one foot inside, before dropping the rest of his weight in, and wincing.

I tried to drive gently. But I could tell that wasn't what the car wanted. It hummed under my hands, and the pedals jumped whenever I applied the slightest pressure. When the car jerked, I'd find myself saying sorry, sorry, to Ian, who would grimace but say nothing.

The restaurant we were assessing that night was called The Gander. He limped towards the door with its gold silhouette of a goose.

He stopped before we went in. 'By the way, don't be too polite.'

'Okay.'

'You know what I mean. Don't be ingratiating. You don't have to care about these people, or worry about their feelings. Just do your job.'

I nodded as though I understood, wondering whether Ian sensed something ingratiating in me, something that needed to be stamped out.

We were greeted and taken to our table. Our waiter was young and pitted with the remains of cystic acne. I could see the comb trails in his gelled red hair. He pulled out Ian's chair, and Ian grasped the waiter's shoulder in order to lower himself.

Once Ian had ordered a bottle of wine, the waiter left us with the menus. Ian's face was scrunched in discomfort. He took a few deep breaths, then looked at me.

'You may as well know. I'm trying to pass a kidney stone. Perhaps several kidney stones.'

He looked me right in the eyes when he said this, as though daring me to discuss it with anything other than a doctor's clinical detachment.

The waiter returned. In a few moments Ian was working chablis around his mouth, energetically, as though it were Listerine. I was thinking of how the waiter, his Adam's apple prominent and bouncing, had described the wine; I remembered the phrase *lingering finish*.

'Will you keep it?' I said.

'Pardon me?'

'The stone. Or stones.'

Ian looked at me sharply.

'I hadn't planned to,' he said. 'No.'

Some smoke arrived under tiny bell jars. The waiter's hands shook as he set them down. The glass jittered. The dish was called Memory of Lamb.

'I read something about people who keep their kidney stones,' I said.

'I don't think I'll want a souvenir.'

'Didn't Benjamin Franklin keep his?'

Ian twisted in his seat, plainly uncomfortable. 'Even so,' he said.

I paused to lift the bell jar. I wasn't sure whether this dish was supposed to make me remember lambs I'd eaten, or whether I was inhaling the memories of an actual lamb.

'They're quite beautiful,' I said. 'Kidney stones. Up close, I mean.'

It was a half-truth that I'd read about people keeping their kidney stones. I'd actually watched a documentary about kidneys during one of my long summer afternoons on the couch waiting for a shift at the call centre. The documentary, part of a series on the human body, showed magnified images of stones people had passed. They were made up of layer upon layer of mineral deposits. They looked like geodes, or something chipped off a coral reef. They glittered when they caught the light.

'People make jewellery out of them,' I told Ian.

'People do all sorts of strange things,' he said.

At the bottom of The Gander's menu, there was a note: *We cook from the heart*. Cooking from the heart, I came to learn, involved a sous-vide machine, and micro herbs applied with tweezers. It involved tongue, basil ice cream, and balsamic in fat, amoeba-ish drops on the plate.

Between one course and another I tried to make conversation. I asked Ian how he had come to be interested in mystery dining.

'Well, I was frequenting restaurants all the time,' he said, pushing his pinky finger into a seared scallop and frowning. 'Mrs Morton wasn't much of a cook. She didn't care for any of the domestic arts, really. Couldn't sew a button on. Couldn't boil an egg. I don't think she could have told you what colour our vacuum cleaner was.'

I twisted some linguini around my fork.

'You remember, don't you? She was always buying profiteroles for Jo's birthday parties because she couldn't sling a sponge cake together.'

'I liked those profiteroles.'

'You must have been a very sophisticated child.'

Ian sat back in his chair, winced, then leaned forward again.

'I know what you're thinking, but I'm not being sexist,' he said. 'I never had a problem with her working, or with putting the girls in childcare. I did my bit around the house. I ironed my shirts. She was just – well, my mother would have said *sluttish*.' He looked at me, trying to judge whether I minded, whether I was shocked. 'In the original sense of the term, of course. A woman of untidy habits and appearance. Slovenly.'

I couldn't think what to say. I chewed and chewed until the food in my mouth had liquefied.

'You like historical tidbits: did you know that a slut was a lard-soaked rag, a sort of primitive lamp, back in the seventeenth century?'

I shook my head.

'It was,' Ian said. 'Look it up.'

———

Ian's assessment was that our waiter should be dismissed from his position. When we returned to the car, he enumerated the boy's faults: he was hesitant, nervous, cringing. He was *servile*.

'Shouldn't waiters be servile?'

'He was the wrong kind of servile. His misery was too visible.'

I pulled out onto the road. Ian grunted and shifted in his seat.

'I thought he was nice,' I said.

'No-one should have to look at a face like that,' Ian replied. 'Not at those prices.'

It was when we were about halfway home that I noticed Ian was squirming. I'd had a glass of wine; Ian had drunk the rest of the bottle. He'd also eaten more than I had – I was surprised by how much he could consume, given how petite he was.

He bent forward, a hand pressed to his side.

'Is everything okay?'

I heard him take a ragged breath.

'Fine,' he said.

I tried to drive slowly, aware in the silence that I could hear him breathing, see the swell of his belly rising and falling. He let out a groan, and then an undisguised trumpet of wind. I kept my eyes trained on the road as the sulphurous odour filled the car.

I took the turnoff and drove up and down the hills over which Ian's suburb was elegantly draped.

When I pulled up outside the house, Ian didn't move. I took the keys out of the ignition.

'Is there – can I do something to help?'

He'd clamped his eyes shut, and when he opened them, there was a lizardish expression on his face as he weighed the severity of his pain against the ignominy of my assistance.

'Maybe just to the door,' he said.

I didn't go home for two weeks.

That first night, I helped him up the driveway, putting my arm around the oversized grey sports coat, smelling the afterglow of restaurant and sulphur that surrounded him.

I was about to turn around and start the long bus journey home when Ian, breathing hard, fumbled with his keys and dropped them.

'Drat,' he said. I went to pick them up but he was quicker; he swooped on the mat where they'd fallen. As he straightened he made a sharp cry, the kind of sound a large, ungainly bird might make.

My first response was alarm. Adrenaline shot through me, and I remembered an image from another in that series of documentaries on the human body: adrenaline, represented as black arrows, firing out of each adrenal gland at atomic speed. We were alone, there under the cobweb-covered light on the verandah. If Ian died, would I be responsible? I looked around to see if anyone was watching.

Finally, he found the right key and opened the door. He heaved his body inside and braced himself against the wall.

I stood on the doormat. He hadn't invited me in.

And he didn't invite me; he just left the door open. Eventually I followed.

He picked his way down the hallway and then lowered himself onto the couch, where he balled up into the foetal position.

'Um, Ian?' I said, his first name feeling strange in my mouth. 'Should I call a doctor?'

He didn't open his eyes. 'No. It will pass.'

'Can I get you anything?'

'There's a box of painkillers in the bathroom cabinet. Second shelf.'

I thought he still had his eyes closed. But when I started moving towards the bathroom he said, 'Not that bathroom. My ensuite.'

I hesitated for a moment, then went to the front of the house and through the master bedroom. I was surprised to see how rumpled it was: a seam of dust on the carpet beneath the windowsill, crumpled tissues on the bedside table, the bed itself extravagantly unmade. *Slovenly*, I thought.

In the ensuite, I opened the cabinet. The pills were exactly where Ian said they would be. I reached out and picked them up. I should have headed back immediately, I knew that. Instead I let the urgency subside. I took a long moment to look around the cabinet, my eyes doing a sweep for anything interesting. There wasn't much: deodorant, floss, antacids, anti-fungal cream, sorbolene. I picked up a hairbrush – it was the expensive boar-bristle kind – and ran my palm over its surface.

When I came back to the living room, Ian was panting.

I handed him the box of pills. He fumbled for the blister pack and popped two out.

'I'll get you some water,' I said.

But he was already chewing the pills, grinding them between his teeth and swallowing. I brought the water anyway. He looked at it, but didn't drink any.

'Should I call someone?' I said. 'I can call Joanna?'

'Absolutely not. Not Annabel either, she has exams.'

He groaned.

'I don't think you should be by yourself,' I said.

He paused, then exhaled forcefully.

'You can stay in Joanna's room,' he said.

Joanna's room hadn't changed since we were teenagers. There were the racks of her shoes, their funk softened by time. Her noticeboard covered with cards and invitations and photographs. She had a king-sized bed, and though the sheets were dusty, they were gloriously soft and comfortable. That first night in the Mortons' house was the best night's sleep I'd had in a long time.

Before I went to sleep, I texted one of my housemates to let her know where I was. She didn't answer. I hardly knew her. I wouldn't be missed.

Later, it occurred to me that I hadn't thought to call Mrs Morton. I wondered whether Ian's condition was something I should tell her about. Would she be concerned – would she pity him? Or would there be a note of schadenfreude in her voice? Though I'd known her for years, I had no idea who she was outside this house. I tried to imagine calling her, but my imagination couldn't come up with anything for her to say. Instead I pictured her holding the phone in silence, a tower of profiteroles hovering nearby.

The next morning Ian called a friend who was a doctor.

I sat in Joanna's room and heard them talking in low voices. There were occasional groans, and one more cry like the one Ian had made at the door. Eventually I was called back into the living room. The friend, a tall, cheerful man with a double chin like a bullfrog's, said, 'It's a good thing you're here.'

Ian was wearing a clean grey tracksuit. He looked red in the face, tinier than ever.

'So you're okay?' I asked.

'Obviously not,' the doctor said before Ian could answer. 'He should have the blasted things removed. But he won't listen to a word I say. Look at him. He's a mule.'

'I'm fine,' Ian said.

'He'll be high as a kite in about ten minutes,' the doctor said, glancing at his watch. 'He'll probably go right to sleep. Ian's told me you've agreed to stay until they're out. Otherwise I would insist he go to a hospital.'

Ian interrupted. 'Thank you, Stephen.'

The doctor gave me his card. 'Call me if he needs me,' he said, and winked.

'I hope it wasn't presumptuous of me to tell him you'd stay,' Ian said once the doctor had gone. 'I will compensate you for your time. That goes without saying.'

'Thank you,' I said, 'It's no problem.'

I hoped he couldn't tell that I was wondering how much compensation I would get.

While in Joanna's room, I'd looked up pictures of kidney stones. I saw one that had been photographed next to a coin, for scale. The thing was almost as big as the coin, and shaped like an arrowhead. I didn't mention this to Ian.

The doctor was not wrong about Ian falling asleep. That day, a bleak, overcast winter day where the windows fogged with condensation, Ian put on the TV and promptly fell asleep in front of it. I was familiar with all the programs and the order in which they unfolded: morning chat show, news, a black and white movie in which everyone was beautiful but not famous enough for me to recognise. Then more news, followed by seventies sitcoms with saturated mustards and oranges and browns.

This is what played in the background while I took the opportunity to make a leisurely tour around the house. I looked through the pantry, the kitchen cabinets, stippled my fingers along the bookshelves. I leafed through some papers on Ian's desk: invoices. I almost laughed when I saw the figures; I would never have that much money in my life.

I wasn't hoping to come across the photos of Mrs Morton – at least that's what I told myself. So I shouldn't have been disappointed that I couldn't find them.

After checking Ian was still deeply asleep, his snores rich and regular, I risked sneaking into his bedroom. I opened the bedside drawer and inventoried the contents with interest: earplugs, Vaporub, an old pair of glasses, more antacids, a yellowed, foxed copy of *The Joy of Sex*.

I sat on the bed and lingered over the illustrations in the book: here was a bearded, shaggy man, here a bemused woman displaying a lush isthmus of underarm hair. Had the Mortons used this book? Had one brusquely read out instructions while the other hauled their knees and hips into position?

By primetime, Ian was sitting up.

'How are you feeling?' I asked.

'Better,' he said. He peeled himself from the couch with difficulty, wiping the drool from his cheek. 'What's for dinner?'

Ian never expressly asked me to be his cleaner or his nurse. The only instruction I'd been given was the doctor's vague request to 'keep an eye on him'. But as the days went by I found myself asked to do more, and to improve the efficiency of my housekeeping. Ian wanted meals at particular times. He wanted his dishes cleared immediately. He noted when I'd failed to use fabric softener, and when I bought the wrong brand of milk. His temper was short, his mood often sour. He would start reading a book and then grow impatient with its weaknesses, which he would describe to me in lavish detail. In his ensuite shower, which he reached by leaning on me, hopping, doing that same odd marionette walk, he would curse loudly. After the water started running I would hear the thuds of shampoo bottles and soap hitting the floor. Later I would clean them up, and pull the hair from the drain.

One day, he called to me.

'Ah, there you are,' he said when I approached the couch. He mopped at his forehead with a tissue. 'I must ask something rather revolting of you.'

Before he could tell me what that was, I saw his bare, dangling feet.

'Clippers are in the ensuite,' he said.

I fetched the clippers and some newspaper, then kneeled in front of him and took his foot in my hand. It was cold and dry, and the nails had grown surprisingly long, curling over the squarish ends of his toes.

'Not too short,' he said, smiling in a way that made his lips so white they were nearly blue.

I clipped his nails as gently as I could while he breathed like a steaming iron, trying and failing to mask the pain he was in. I wondered whether the stones were trying to work their way out. I wondered how large they were, and what shape, and whether I'd one day walk into the ensuite to see them gathered in the porcelain bowl like tiny little treasures I could scoop up and keep.

How did I amuse myself through those long invalid days? Usually I would wait for Ian to fall asleep, then change the channel, or read one of the books he'd cast aside.

Eventually I decided to try to prune the monstera. It would be easy enough to do: the advice I'd read on forums was that the more savage you are, the better.

I went to the shed and retrieved long-handled secateurs, thinking I'd settle for clearing away the scorched or yellowing leaves, anything dead or dying. But once I started, it was hard to stop. I kept clipping and clipping until only the denuded spine of the monstera was left. Then I started snipping away at this central stem, chewing through the woodier parts with the secateurs until it had all come away in vertebrae-sized chunks.

I cleaned up the mess and went inside, dirty, sweating. Ian was watching me. I wondered how much he'd witnessed.

'Is it gone?' he said.

I glanced out the window. 'Looks that way.'

'Good,' he said. 'Good riddance.'

It was soon after this that I had to call Ian's doctor.

Ian had been in the ensuite shower. I'd been at the kitchen sink, using a fingernail to scrape the tines of a fork. I heard one of the customary thuds, and then another thud. Much louder, much heavier, and accompanied by a sound closer to a scream than a groan. I gripped the fork and didn't move.

After a minute, his plaintive voice floated down the hallway. 'Susie?'

I turned, but didn't answer.

'Susie?' Louder this time, more desperate.

I walked as gently as I could to the bedroom, letting the carpet absorb the sound. I pressed my ear to the door. At first I heard only the running water, but then I made out other sounds: little huffs of breath, something that could have been a sob.

I knocked. I called, 'Ian? Are you all right in there?'

The door was unlocked. I went in. He was curled over in the shower recess, beyond shame. I didn't intend to look at his genitals, but found myself glancing there anyway. All I saw was something pink receding into its thick nest of grey hair. I opened the glass door, turned off the taps, cast a towel over his body, and helped Ian to his feet.

But before I did any of those things, I slid my phone from my pocket and took a photograph. Ian's eyes were closed. He was too distracted by his agony to notice.

'Come on,' I said once he was standing. I wrapped the towel around his shoulders the way you might wrap a child. He leaned against me, shivering. 'Come on. You're okay. It's going to be okay.'

'I knew this would happen,' the doctor said when I called. 'Stubborn old prick. Give me half an hour.'

After I hung up I went to the sofa where Ian was lying and crouched next to him. I couldn't dress him on my own, so had arranged several towels around him as artfully as I could. Sweat had curled the hair at the nape of his neck. He was red in the face, clammy. His eyes were shut.

'Call him back,' he said. He was shaking. 'Tell him I'm fine.'

I shook my head. 'I wish I could.'

'I'll pay you,' he said without opening his eyes. 'How much? How much do you want?'

I put my hand on his forehead. 'You're burning up.'

He drew his knees further towards his chest. 'You're fired,' he said.

We waited together for the doctor, the midday movie muted on TV. I stroked Ian's hair as I knelt beside him. I turned my face towards the screen and watched the film in silence – two beautiful people I didn't recognise were dancing. I watched their faces, I watched their lips moving, but I couldn't tell whether they loved or despised one another.

Beyond the TV was the razed monstera. I wouldn't be here to see it revive. But I liked to think of Ian convalescing on the couch, watching the plant as it came back to life. I liked to think of it creeping along the side of his house and worming in through the windows and under the doors, dropping new roots as it went. I liked to think of Ian seeing the new leaves uncurl and turn to the sun, broad and glossy, content in their ugliness. I thought with great pleasure of the shadow they would cast.

Frogs' Legs

Even the sunsets are dirty here.

I've taken to smoking in the swimming pool, floating on my back with my ears underwater, keeping out the sounds of the traffic. The colours are all there, as glorious as they're supposed to be: gold and fuchsia and tangerine. But between me and them there's a tacky, brown-grey film, like something you'd wipe off a bar.

At least smoking repels the insects. Some nights I swim to the side of the pool and flick ash at them, watching the tiny sparks fly through the air.

I stopped taking my malaria tablets weeks ago.

I prefer to have the pool to myself. It's a perfect circle, white with stripes of grime and rust. When I'm floating in the middle, I feel like the pupil in a bloodshot eye.

But there's a man who joins me in the evenings.

He swims a languid breaststroke around the perimeter: once, twice, maybe a dozen times. Then he sits on one of the ladders and lets the water lap at his belly, which is taut and round and hairy, like a coconut.

Some nights I sit on the pool's edge and watch him swim. He kicks his skinny legs like a frog.

I've eaten the local frogs. There isn't much meat on them, but I like to throw the bones to the street dogs. When the dogs approach I stroke them and scratch behind their ears, despite their sores, their limps, their stink. 'Good boy,' I murmur as they wag their tails. 'Good boy.'

I was supposed to get a rabies shot before I came here, but I didn't.

One night I was sitting on the edge of the pool and the man was sitting on a ladder. He asked for a cigarette, and I used the tip of mine to light it for him.

We sat in silence, smoking, flicking ash at the mosquitoes.

I found myself wondering what would happen if I fucked this man. I would insist we went to his room, not mine. I would have him lie flat on his back to make sure his gut was out of the way. I wondered whether he'd have a condom and whether I'd ask him to use it.

And afterwards: would he be the sort of man to flush it? Or would he slide it off and let it drop to the floor?

Then I wondered: if I were a dog, would I eat him? I thought of the dogs I feed here, of their bald pink patches, their dusty eyes, the way I've seen them lap hopefully at plastic. They would eat him without hesitation.

The man ground his cigarette out against the pool's edge. He'd only smoked half of it. I watched as he slapped a mosquito and checked his hand for blood.

Yes, I thought. I'd eat him. But only the best parts, the softest parts. The rest I'd leave for dogs who were truly starving; dogs a little hungrier than me.

Hold Your Fire

While waiting for his faecal transplant, my husband wasn't as fun as he used to be. This was largely due to the changes in his diet. He had to be strict. He was down to eating chicken breasts poached in unseasoned water, and a small variety of baby vegetables. Baby carrots, baby corn, baby beets.

'Why only baby vegetables? How is baby corn different from corn?' I was being peevish. I couldn't help myself.

'It's what the doctor said. I can't take any chances.'

I stared while he cut the piece of baby corn into three, chewing each piece the recommended twenty-five times. I actually counted the movements of his jaw. Twenty-five, right on the money, every time.

I knew that I should take his condition more seriously. The last time Connor had thrown caution to the wind – it was his birthday, he ate a chicken parmigiana and a tiramisu and nearly wept with the joy of it – he'd had to run home from the train station the next morning because, without warning and in considerable volume, he'd shat his pants.

He'd grown wan like a wilting lily on this new diet. It wasn't just the pallor and the weight loss, which left him looking bent, like his head was too heavy for his body. It was that he'd lost shape and definition, muscle mass. I felt I might accidentally skim a bit of him off, the way you can chip part of a mushroom away without really meaning to.

To make matters worse, he had become obsessed not only with his condition, but with its accoutrements. The most prized among these was a footstool he used to make evacuation more comfortable. It had been recommended to him in a faecal forum. Rather than a simple plastic stool that could be purchased anywhere, he invested in an ergonomic timber one; comfortable, warm, but still easy to clean. The forum had a preferred artisan who took Connor's foot size and height into consideration. Connor loved that stool. Whenever we went away for the weekend it came with us in the car.

'Anyway. Tell me about your day,' I said, spinning my glass of wine. I'd given up joining him in his misery, and was halfway through a bloody steak.

Connor addressed our son, Samuel. 'We went to the park,' he said. 'Didn't we?'

Samuel nodded enthusiastically. 'Daddy saved a seagull.'

'He did?' I knew I sounded sarcastic, but Samuel didn't seem to notice.

'It was hurt,' he said.

'I just called the council.' Connor cut his chicken breast along the grain. 'Poor thing couldn't fly. It was the least I could do.'

I could tell he wanted to be congratulated for his humane behaviour, for the good example he was setting.

'They'll just euthanise it, you know,' I said. 'Kinder to let the other birds kill it.'

They would, too. I'd seen the way those gulls went at each other.

Samuel looked at me, appalled. He got up from the table and ran to his father. Connor bent his head to Samuel and I wished, once again, that Connor wasn't going bald. He looked like a villainous, wispy invalid, the more so because his paleness made the rims around his eyes seem a bright watery red, like tomato skins.

Connor put his arm around Samuel and hushed him.

'You said seagull would get better,' Samuel said. Then he commenced whimpering.

This annoyed me. Samuel was a smart child – smart enough to understand the word 'euthanise' – and he knew where to put a definite article. He reverted to baby talk to soften up my husband. This was unnecessary. If Connor were any softer you'd be able to eat him with a spoon.

'Mummy doesn't mean it,' Connor said, looking over him to meet my eye. 'Mummy's had a hard day at work. She's very tired.'

Mummy was two glasses of wine down and hadn't had satisfactory penetrative sex in more than a year.

'Daddy's right,' I said. I drained my glass. 'Mummy's very tired.'

I liked Samuel best when he was asleep, though even then his drooling and the curl of his little marsupial hands irritated me. No-one had told me it was possible to dislike your child. Or at least, if you did, it was supposed to happen later, when they were bratty teenagers and then ungrateful, smug adults. I didn't like Samuel right off the bat. Don't get me wrong – I loved him, in the sense that I had every intention of discharging my obligations towards him – but to be frank, he was annoying.

He was fussy, for a start, fussy about temperature and sunlight and noise. He had a series of illogical phobias: he was scared of denim and windscreen wipers, and would scream if he could smell bananas. When he danced he used moves that were weirdly sophisticated, even risqué – rolling his body, thrusting his hips – things he must have dragged up out of the collective unconscious, because he certainly didn't see me or Connor dance like that, or at all. In some ways I was looking forward to the inevitable bullying he'd receive. I was hoping that the cruelty of other children would effect developmental changes that I couldn't seem to trigger.

Worsening all of this was the fact that Connor seemed oblivious. He took no responsibility for his part in creating a defective human being.

One night, in bed, I'd tried to talk to him about it.

'Do you think Samuel's a little …'

I was hoping I wouldn't have to finish the sentence.

'A little what?'

I rolled my eyes in the darkness.

'What?' Connor hissed. He still had some grit about him then. He wasn't spending his days on forums, trying to chat up faecal donors.

'You know. You know what I mean.'

'You're talking about our son here.'

'I know that.'

'And there's nothing wrong with him. He's perfect just as he is.'

'Okay, geez,' I said. 'No need to get defensive.'

I rolled over.

Maybe I was able to view things more objectively because I'd thought Samuel was off since he'd been a foetus. He'd felt like an alien in there, wriggling around, eating my lunch, kicking my organs. Connor wouldn't understand. Tapeworms are less intrusive.

It was a relief to get to work in the mornings. I made excuses about having to be in early, about my boss being demanding, but the truth was that my boss was a sanguine, paunchy man with a lunch budget of a hundred thousand dollars a year, who sauntered around humming Ravel's *Bolero* or selections from the musical *Chess*. My name is Fiona but he called me Fifi. He had twelve grandchildren and was the one I ended up confiding in about Samuel, about my suspicions that I disliked him as a person.

'Don't worry,' he'd advised. 'You're allowed to have favourites.'

He then told me how he'd ranked his own grandchildren in order of preference. At the top of the list was Maisie, eight, who wore a severe side part and had won the role of Mary in the previous year's Christmas pageant, despite strong campaigning from the parents of two other girls. At the bottom of the list was Eden, five, who had once eaten a bar of soap.

'I mean the whole thing,' Roger said. 'He didn't eat a bit and stop. He ate the entire thing. Was burping bubbles.'

Eden had also dropped his pants in the school playground, unprompted. Roger worried that this might be an indicator of future depravity.

'I've told my son: Drive to the middle of the bush and push him out of the car. He won't listen. Doesn't listen to a word I say.'

He was joking, of course. My office was full of the nicest people I'd ever known. I worked for Raleigh, one of the largest defence, aerospace and security companies in the world. I had a PhD in engineering. I'd spent a number of relatively measly years in the university's engineering department, working on robots, or what passed for robots; nothing that was going to pass the Turing test. We'd had to scramble and scheme for every grant, every dollar of funding, and I had to renew my contract every six months. I felt like one of those seagulls fighting over the cold chips thrown by tourists. People were only too happy to enter into bitter, decades-long feuds. These fights were often the only thing sustaining their work after the money and accolades dried up.

At Raleigh, there were no such problems. It was nice to be where the real money was. There was plenty for everyone and so the atmosphere was genial. I'd never known such camaraderie as I found when I started designing weapons for a living.

I was part of the air-to-air missile team. We were working on an updated version of our signature AAM, the Raleigh Starling, refining the design and placement of the attitude thrusters – tiny, outward-facing rockets that fired when the missile needed to change course.

In the longer term, Raleigh hoped to develop a missile that could turn in midair and fly back to its target at more or less the same speed. The goal was to increase the no-escape zone. This is exactly what it sounds like, and was a selling point when it came to taking our product to Poland, the UK, Kuwait, Japan, Qatar.

Roger had no qualms whatsoever about designing weapons that could cause massive, instant carnage. I knew this because, unprompted, he told me. It was my first week, and I was in the staff kitchen heating noodles in the microwave. He was on his way back from lunch. He stuck his head into the room.

'I think your ramen days are over, don't you?'

I looked at the spinning bowl, thought of the invisible waves causing the molecules to go haywire.

'It's good to stay humble. Isn't it?'

He scoffed at this.

'Don't ever be ashamed,' he said. 'Not of the work, the money – none of it. That's what the little people want. To shame you. They don't understand.'

He came close and his voice was low and conspiratorial. Even his halitosis smelled expensive, like beurre blanc and fennel.

'The way I see it,' he said, 'it's like karate. You learn karate so that you never have to use it. And no-one looks askance at a man for learning karate, do they?'

I had to agree; they didn't.

'That's the thing you need to remember, Fifi,' Roger said, pleased with his own wisdom. 'Everyone holds their fire. It might come down to the last minute, the last second even. But no-one really wants to press the button.'

I told Connor about this view of my new position, and he was only too happy to agree.

I'd thought he would disapprove of my working at Raleigh. But weeks earlier, when I told him about the offer I'd received, and how much I'd be paid, he said, 'Sounds great.'

I was surprised. 'Really?'

Connor had briefly been an anarchist, and also a vegetarian. He'd gone through a period of wearing Nehru shirts. Now he was a marketing consultant, but still – I hadn't expected so little resistance.

'Someone's going to do it, right?'

'Sure.'

'May as well be you.'

I had been gearing up for a fight, and found myself disappointed I wasn't going to get one.

'You don't mind? Truly?'

He was reading the ingredients on a tub of yoghurt. He didn't answer me. This was just when his digestive problems were turning serious. He peeled the foil lid away from the yoghurt and licked it.

'I have a feeling I'm going to regret this,' he said.

The call came to me because Connor was at an appointment. The appointment was about his faecal transplant, or FMT as he'd taken to calling it. The difficulty he had – the reason he'd been waiting so long – was that FMTs were usually only given to people infected by the stubborn C. diff bacteria. People could die from C. diff infections, Connor told me during one of his long, stuttering bouts on our ensuite toilet. But faecal transplants were an exceptionally effective treatment; the healthy bacteria in the donor stool could wipe out the infection. Rates of success were as high as 95 per cent.

It wasn't easy to get an FMT, though, if you weren't being treated for C. diff. Even Connor's particularly volatile IBS didn't make him an ideal candidate. Doctors were unwilling or unable – Connor was evasive on this point – to refer him to a colonoscopy centre to have the procedure.

That day, he was seeing a new doctor, armed with his own research and an email exchange with a man he'd met on Poop4You.com. Connor had seen the man's screening results and described his stool as 'pristine'. He'd offered the man two hundred dollars for a donation and he had agreed.

When the phone at my desk rang it shocked me out of my reverie. I'd been eating salad and reading an article in *Munitions Journal* about recent constraints in the AAM market. 'Constraints' meant that one war or another had come to an end. Our shares would rise when another one started.

I picked up the phone. 'Fiona Tomlinson.'

'Fiona? Hi, it's Gaby from Blossomings.'

This was the preposterously named early-learning centre that Samuel attended.

'Hello,' I said. I looked at my half-eaten salad and *Munitions Journal* wistfully.

'I'm sorry if this is a bad time. It's just that – well, we have something of a situation.'

'I've told you before, Samuel's not really allergic to bananas, no matter what he says. He's just scared of them.'

'It's not bananas.'

'His sunglasses should be in his bag, if it's the light thing again.'

'No, it's not his photosensitivity. There's been an incident with one of our other pupils.'

This got my attention. 'Oh?'

'I mean, Samuel's okay, he's fine, he's just —'

I let the journal fall closed. 'Just what?'

'I think he should go home for the day. Could you come and collect him?'

'Did someone hurt my son?'

'Mrs Tomlinson —'

'Dr Tomlinson.'

There was a fractional pause.

'*Doctor* Tomlinson. I understand that you might find this an upsetting situation, but I'm here to assure you that at Blossomings, we —'

I hung up and grabbed my keys.

'It's my son,' I said to Roger on the way out. 'He needs to be picked up from day care. Something's happened.'

'Oh God,' said Roger. I started to walk away and my boss's voice followed me down the corridor. 'Did he keep his pants on?'

Blossomings was painted in muted shades that recalled nature: greens and browns, occasional bursts of autumnal orange. It was designed to be calming. Theirs was an 'expansive' style of education – like a Steiner school, but without the insanity. They let the children play with paint and pipe cleaners, but also introduced them to a few words in Mandarin and taught them to mash their little fists on electric pianos. It was ludicrously expensive, of course, but we were at the point where this gave us relief rather than anxiety; it was good to think that Samuel was surrounded by people who would be influential in the future. He was going to need all the help he could get.

I started heading for Samuel's classroom – his 'experience pod' – but Gaby came out and met me in the corridor. Nature sounds – dripping water, breezes through trees, bird calls – floated past us, putting us at ease and allowing us to enter our most creative and receptive states.

'Where is he?'

'Dr Tomlinson, it's so nice to see you. Thank you for coming in. Samuel's fine.'

'Where is he? What happened?'

'Everything's fine.'

'What happened?'

'Why don't you have a seat?'

She gestured to an undulating green bench. I didn't sit.

'So help me God, Gaby, if you don't tell me *right now* what the fuck is going on …' Spittle was flying from my mouth as I enunciated my consonants. My winter coat had cost over a thousand dollars – it swished in what I liked to think of as an authoritative fashion around my knees.

There was a pause, and we heard a kookaburra singing. Gaby looked around to make sure no-one had witnessed my outburst.

'This way,' she said.

Samuel was asleep in the sick bay, which Blossomings called the 'wellness centre'. We stood in a kind of anteroom filled with low children's chairs and educational toys made from felt and wood, and looked in on him through the window, as if he were in quarantine. There was a bandaid on his chin. Blossomings used bandaids derived from bamboo.

'If he has any lasting damage —'

'Dr Tomlinson, we can assure you, it's just a little graze. Barely noticeable. He's really here because he needed some space to calm down.'

'He needed to *calm down*? *He* needed to calm down?'

'What I mean is —'

The door from the corridor opened. We turned to see a frumpy woman coming in, early forties, wearing depressing earth-mother-ish clothing – some sort of thermal skivvy stretched over the welcoming expanse of her bosom, a thick elastic headband, a tunic that was probably made of hemp. Her shoes were red and fastened with Velcro. Her leggings had stripes. Her rosacea added another level of clash to the overall ensemble.

'Are you the nurse?' I said. She looked like someone who might work at Blossomings.

'You must be Samuel's mother,' she said, glancing at Gaby. 'Dr Tomlinson – is that right?'

When I assented, she said, 'I hope I'm not interrupting?'

'Oh no, not at all, Deidre,' said Gaby. When Gaby smiled, you could see more gum than tooth. It was off-putting. 'I was just going to come and ask you to join the conversation.'

'Why don't you sit down?' Deidre said to me.

'Who are you?'

Her smile was indulgent. 'Deidre Moss,' she said. 'Luna's mother.'

'Luna?'

'She's in Samuel's pod. They found themselves a little out of sync today.'

'Out of *sync*?' I was trying to be outraged, but found myself sitting in one of the children's chairs, my coat's hem limp on the ground, the toes of my pumps pointing at one another. My handbag was in my lap.

Deidre sat too. She reached out and touched my arm. 'They're so mysterious, kids. Aren't they? They have their own little worlds. Who can keep up?'

Her face was so close that I could see all the broken veins, like little purple lightning forks, in the ruddy terrain of her skin. I felt my anger collapse in on itself; I couldn't get it out. It felt like my throat was closing over.

'Are you feeling okay, Dr Tomlinson?' Deidre asked. She stroked my arm. 'Do you want some water? Gaby, could you be an angel and fetch Dr Tomlinson some water?'

Gaby was only too happy to leave the room. 'Of course,' she said, flashing her gums. 'Take your time.'

Deidre sat back in her chair, using the expanse of her gut as a kind of armrest.

'He's a beautiful little kid,' she said. 'Sammy. Just gorgeous.'

No-one had ever called him Sammy.

I felt fuzzy-headed; I was struggling to remember why we were there. It was those nature sounds. They were getting under my skin. This was why I didn't trust relaxation of any kind.

'Hm,' was all I could manage.

She leaned towards me. Something she'd applied to her body contained a high percentage of ylang-ylang.

'I've told Connor over and over. Sammy's a gem. Such a funny little kid. Such an original.' She clucked with laughter at a private memory of some amusement my son had afforded her.

Gaby came back in and gave me a biodegradable cup filled with chilled water that had had the fluoride filtered out. With her was a dour, strawberry-blonde child with a downturned mouth and chubby cheeks. I had to admit it: the child was adorable.

'Look who I found!' said Gaby.

'Luna-bear,' said Deidre. The child wandered over with a strange, knowing weariness and flopped her weight into the pillow of her mother's belly. 'There you are.'

The child stared at me.

'I think,' said Gaby, joining us in the circle of tiny chairs, 'now that everyone's here, we ought to talk about what happened today. Just so everyone's feeling okay about it. How does that sound?'

'With the child here?' I said.

'Of course,' said Deidre. 'This concerns her. She should be part of the conversation. Feel free to bring Sammy in. If you're happy for him to be woken up.'

We all gazed into the other room, where Samuel slept, untroubled.

Deidre's fingernails were stumpy and cuticles sprang up from their sides. I directed my gaze away from her and towards her daughter. I looked Luna square in her pale blue eyes. I remembered reading somewhere that the most common eye colour for murderers is pale blue. I wasn't going to let this child intimidate me.

'You're in big trouble,' I said.

'Now just a moment —' said Gaby.

'It's all right,' said Deidre. She held up her hand and Gaby stopped talking. Luna stared up at her. 'Remember what we said about having difficult conversations?'

Luna nodded, though whether she had any comprehension of what Deidre said remained unclear.

'Good girl. Why don't you tell Dr Tomlinson what happened?'

'I punched him,' Luna said then.

'You did *what*?'

I hadn't expected her to be so blunt.

'Wait, let's regroup,' Gaby said. 'Remember what you told me, Luna? You said you and Sammy were just playing.'

Luna didn't blink. 'I punched him,' she said again. She stood away from her mother and mimed an uppercut. It was graceful, a sickle-swipe up through the air. 'I punched him like that.'

'And what did he do that made you respond physically?' said Deidre, her voice full of understanding.

'I don't care about her motivations,' I said. I could feel my temper hit a rolling boil. 'She's four. What kind of reason do you expect her to give?'

'She's three, actually,' Deidre said. Luna had returned to her and Deidre was stroking her long, smooth hair. 'Blossomings felt she wasn't being sufficiently challenged in the lower age pod. She's been accelerated.'

'Uplifted,' Gaby corrected.

'Uplifted,' Deidre repeated. 'Anyway – go on, honey.'

'We were playing goodies and baddies,' said Luna. 'He was the baddy.'

'You see? A simple case of misplaced verisimilitude,' Deidre said. 'She must have read about so-called "goodies" and "baddies" somewhere. I don't allow screen time, obviously, but I don't like to censor her taste in books.'

'Sammy's fine, truly,' Gaby chimed in.

'Samuel,' I said.

'He's the baddy,' Luna said.

'This is fucking ridiculous,' I said, before I could stop myself.

Luna's face was gleeful. 'She said a bad word, Mummy,' she said, her blue eyes on me. 'Is she a bad lady?'

'No, sweetheart,' said Deidre. 'She's just upset. And when people are upset they find it hard to control their feelings.'

Samuel chose that moment to appear at the door.

'Mum?'

'Come here, darling,' I said. 'Let me take a look at you.'

He looked wary at my effusiveness, and I didn't blame him. But, through loyalty or lack of imagination, he obeyed.

I tilted his chin up, examined his face with its oddly proportioned features that I hoped would grow into some semblance of harmony.

'Do you have a headache?' I asked.

He looked at me hard, trying to figure out the answer I wanted.

'Yes,' he said.

'How many fingers am I holding up?' I held up two.

Samuel looked at me, his eyes searching.

Come on, I thought.

'Four,' he said.

On the way home we stopped at McDonald's. I bought us both ice-cream sundaes with extra chocolate topping.

'Don't tell your father,' I said.

He promised he wouldn't. We sat in companionable silence in one of the booths, scratching the sides of our cups with plastic spoons, scraping up every iota of lactose we could get.

In bed that night: another whispered conversation with Connor. I don't know why we whispered; Samuel's room was downstairs. But that was how these talks happened, as though someone were listening, as though they might not approve of what they heard.

'He could have been concussed,' I said.

'But he wasn't.'

'He could have been.'

'He's fine. Aren't you the one who says we should be teaching him resilience?'

'That's exactly what I'm doing. This little bitch came for him and I'm teaching him not to back down.'

'Jesus Christ. She's what – four years old? You really need to let this go.'

I didn't tell him Luna's real age.

'Someone punched our son and you want me to let it go? What the fuck is the matter with you?'

'Nothing. God. I just think you should pick your battles.'

'I do. I pick this one.'

He sighed for dramatic effect in the darkness. I'd demanded that Samuel receive a medical examination, that there be an investigation into Luna's behaviour and Gaby's negligence. I'd felt strangely exalted there in the anteroom, making my list of demands. The rage had been white-hot. I'd had the distinct sense that this was how a mother *should* feel, that for once I was getting it right. At home, I'd sent the director of Blossomings a strongly worded email. I wouldn't stop until Luna was expelled from Blossomings. I would make sure she was kept out of every good school. I would hunt down her university applications and see them rejected. I would phone her future employers. I'd show up at her wedding, bristling with objections.

'Try to remember she's just a child,' Connor said.

'Can you grow a spine for a second, please? You're supposed to be on my side.'

'I am on your side.'

'Are you in love with Deidre? Is that it? You want to put her floppy tit in your mouth?'

'What? Where did that come from?'

'You want to bury your face in her bush? I bet it's a big one, Connor. I bet it goes all the way to her knees.'

'Christ, Fiona. I wish you could hear yourself sometimes.'

'Have you seen her rosacea?'

'I'm going to sleep.'

Roger, thankfully, was on my side.

'Hippies,' he said, giving a little *humph* of derision. 'It always descends into violence with them, doesn't it?'

We thought we'd come up with an innovative new placement for attitude thrusters, one that might improve their ability to direct the Starling's course. We were waiting for the prototype to be built so that testing could begin. It was a long process, and while it was happening Roger was on edge. If we failed, he would be the one answering questions, explaining the budget, justifying our choices.

He was only too happy to have a distraction.

'Tell him to hit her back,' he said.

'I thought of that. But she's a girl.'

'Doesn't really matter at that age. Some girls nowadays are monstrously big. It's the hormones in chicken, they think. All these little overdeveloped girls with huge feet, wearing training bras before they're in primary school – a disgrace, if you ask me. Maisie's chicken intake is supervised very closely. We're thinking of moving her to game birds. Pheasant, quail, that sort of thing.'

We were sitting in his office. He had a whiteboard on the wall with NO-ESCAPE ZONE written on it, circled in red. We both wore beautiful suits. His was navy, his shirt blue, his tie white and wet because he'd spilled jus on it at lunch and rinsed it in the bathroom.

'What about insults – has he tried those? Is she fat? Ugly? Stupid?'

'I don't think so.'

'Kids don't have to be PC. If she's slow, or deaf, or has an overbite or something he can say it – he's got carte blanche, really. He should take advantage while he can.'

'I've told him to ignore her.'

'Well, that never works.'

'I've written a letter to the centre.'

He laughed outright at this, a big expulsion of garlic-scented air.

'Goodness me. It's like you want him to be picked on,' he said. 'Seriously, Fifi. Take him aside, and show him how to kick her in the shins.'

Blossomings sent me a very polite and very thorough letter in response to my concerns. They thanked me for taking the time to write. They remarked upon what a special little boy Samuel was, and how they cherished him, as did his classmates. They said they took my complaint very seriously, and after an internal review and lengthy discussions with all involved, had decided that no further action needed to be taken.

I tore the letter up, enjoying the feeling of the heavy, recycled stock they used coming apart in my hands.

I wasn't sure what to do next. I supposed I would have to settle for biding my time.

One night, Connor brought me a glass of wine after he'd bathed Samuel and put him to bed. He rubbed my shoulders.

'That's nice,' I said. I leaned my head back against his body, enjoying the pressure of his thumbs against the knots in my shoulders. I'd found part of a parsley stalk between my teeth and was idly grinding it into a pulp.

'God, you're so tense, babe,' Connor said. 'You really need to relax.'

Easy for him to say. Due to his IBS, he now mostly worked from home, spending the days in tracksuit pants – a garment that could be quickly lowered and easily laundered.

'I am relaxed.'

'Shh,' he said, 'shhhh.'

I felt my neck lock up. He took my silence for compliance.

'Just breathe,' he said.

Connor never used to say such idiotic things. It was those faecal forums. They were full of people who bought salt lamps and slept with lumps of quartz under their pillows.

'I am breathing.'

'Try counting to five on the inhale.'

'Connor —'

'It really helps.'

I knew he was trying to be nice. *Nice.* The word set my teeth on edge.

'That sort of thing never works for me.'

'You never try it. Come on.'

I realised that my toes in their nylons had actually curled; in distaste, in embarrassment. But I couldn't stand the plea in his voice. With great effort I did as he asked, breathing in and out for five counts each.

'There,' he said. 'Don't you feel better?'

I was imagining Luna's uppercut. The unfortunate truth was that I envied her the freedom to make that punch. I imagined it felt wonderful when it connected. I couldn't remember the last time I'd allowed my body to express how I genuinely felt. The stiffness, the tension of keeping myself from doing or saying what I wanted, was as close to authentic expression as I was able to get. As I breathed, I imagined my own fist connecting with Deidre's chin.

Inhale.

Exhale.

Inhale.

Exhale.

'You know what?' I said to Connor. 'You were right. I do feel better.'

In the weeks that followed, Samuel reported nothing about Luna. Connor would drop him off, pick him up. I'd get a solemn *ni hao* from him, and the occasional picture made from muddy-coloured pieces of felt. Everyone seemed to have forgotten the entire incident.

I didn't have to go near Blossomings again until Connor went in for his transplant. He had found a specialist centre willing to provide the service for IBS 'on an experimental basis'. Connor was disheartened to learn that he wouldn't be able to select his own donor. The clinic insisted on using their own donors, who were thoroughly screened according to a protocol that Connor perused with reluctant approval. Apparently they dropped off their donations in the morning on the way to work, like chickens delivering their own freshly laid eggs.

'Still,' he said, 'I'd like to know who my donor is. It's personal. They'll become a part of me.'

He said this without a shred of amusement. I made non-committal noises and cracked the top on a bottle of wine.

Connor would be in the FMT centre for half a day. His procedure time clashed with the time Samuel needed to be picked up.

That afternoon I looked around the Blossomings carpark, but Deidre and her hefty shoes were nowhere to be seen.

Samuel came out, sluggish and wet-lipped as ever. He was swinging his book bag.

'Good day?' I said.

He nodded. He told me he was a wizard and also a dinosaur. I told him that would present certain logistical difficulties.

We drove into traffic. It was drizzly, humid; I could feel my hair frizzing at my temples and smoothed it to no avail.

I cleared my throat and glanced at him in the rear-view mirror. 'How's Luna?' I said.

'Good.'

'Is she a wizard too?'

'No.'

'A dinosaur?'

'She's a fairy.'

I nearly snorted at this.

'Has she hit you again?'

'No.'

'Are you sure?'

A sullen nod, exaggerated, which gave him a momentary double chin. I could see how much he resembled Connor.

'You can tell me if she did. You don't have to lie. I won't be mad.'

'I like Luna,' he said. Then he added, matter-of-factly, 'I'm going to marry her.'

Perhaps some mothers would have laughed, or found this adorable; perhaps that's what Samuel was expecting. I doubt he could have understood the rage his remark fired in me. All at once I was picturing Luna in a wedding photo on my wall, Luna pushing my redheaded, potato-faced grandchild on a creaking swing set, Luna picking over my jewellery as I lay on my deathbed. Luna, breasts wobbling in their training bra, jamming her huge feet into all my beautiful shoes.

The transplant didn't work. Or rather, it worked briefly, for a couple of weeks, and then Connor got a little overconfident. He'd begun cautiously, eating a piece of white bread, a slice of cheese, eating – to Samuel's horror – a banana. But this moderation didn't last long. Soon Connor was drinking craft beer, eating tubs of choc-chip ice cream, joining me in my glasses of wine and bloody steaks.

'Are you okay?' I asked one night. 'Are you sure?'

He had a forkful of buttery mashed potato.

'Never better,' he said. He pronounced the treatment a miracle. In his most evangelical moments he proposed writing a book about his experience with FMT in order to raise awareness and diminish stigma. I encouraged him in this, or at least I didn't discourage him. Not because I thought the poop-awareness memoir would ever eventuate, but because he was better with a little iron in his blood, happier, more active. One night he even managed a hopeful erection, which he prodded – its tip oddly cool – into my buttock. It was too fleeting to seize, but still: it gave us hope.

Two days later, however, the run of good times ended. Connor was back in the ensuite, squirming and groaning.

He returned to his diet of poached chicken and baby vegetables, his suspicion of fibre and sugar, his hyper-vigilance regarding toxins. Strangely – so strangely I didn't feel I could mention it to him – the smell of his stool, or at least what was left lingering in the bathroom, was different. I didn't realise I had known his smell, but I did, and this wasn't it. This wasn't a stink of ours. This was the stench of an interloper.

Not long after this, Connor called me at work. I declined the call and texted him: *I'm in a meeting.*

I wasn't in a meeting. I was staring at a page of someone else's equations, looking for errors.

Urgent, Connor wrote.

'For fuck's sake,' I said to no-one in particular, and went into the corridor to call him.

'I've just stepped out,' I said when he picked up.

'It's Samuel,' he said.

'Oh Christ.' I made my voice a whisper. 'Did he drop his pants?'

'He – what? No! God, why would you say that?'

'I don't know.'

'No, he's had a fall. He's fine, he's fine, I've picked him up. They wanted us to come in for a conference, but it's fine, I've handled it.'

'A conference?'

'I didn't think it was necessary.'

'What kind of conference?'

'With the school.'

I gave him a moment to provide me with a more complete answer. When he didn't, I said, 'The school? And who else?'

I heard him exhale.

'And Deidre Moss.'

I closed my eyes, felt the fury swirling in my body, saw the inside of my eyelids turn red.

'It's that little cunt of a daughter of hers, isn't it?'

I was enjoying myself.

'What the fuck's she done this time?'

Connor's voice was flat. 'He says she pushed him off the top of a slide.'

'You don't believe him?'

'I think it was an accident.' He paused. A long pause. 'You know what he's like.'

I was silent for a second, winded almost. I thought of all the effort I'd put into not only making Samuel, but maintaining his existence. No-one, not even Connor, had any concept of the work it took, the exertion, the sacrifice, the tedium, the indignity. How *dare* he?

'Fiona? You there?'

'I'm here.' My voice was calm.

'I'm sure it was just an accident,' Connor said again. I pictured him rubbing the back of his neck, a self-soothing gesture that never failed to rile me.

'Is that what you're going to say when we're lowering his little casket into the ground?' I liked the sound of my voice: cool, controlled, an octave deeper.

'Fiona —'

'Better start on that eulogy, Connor. Here, let me help. "Today we bury our sort-of beloved son Samuel, and let me say I am so thrilled that Deidre Moss has made the time to be here."'

'For the last time, I'm not in love with Deidre fucking Moss!'

It occurred to me then that I wouldn't care if Connor and

Deidre were having an affair. I wouldn't care if Connor was having an affair at all. It would have been like hearing that your teddy bear held parties while you were out.

Connor exhaled heavily. 'Why do you have to see the worst in everything? Why can't you accept that it might have been totally innocent?'

'Don't be so naive.'

'She's a *child*.' He stopped, preparing himself for one of his rare bursts of courage. 'Besides, can't you let me handle this? Can't you support me in anything? You're supposed to be my wife!'

I laughed at this. I could see Roger coming back from lunch. We smiled and waved at one another, and as he passed, I caught the scent of something rich and beefy.

'Don't be ridiculous,' I said. 'If anything, you're my wife.'

I hung up.

I called Blossomings and said yes, we would like to have a conference. They arranged for it to be held after hours in the office of the director, Ms Simon. We left Samuel in a supervised play area, where he took up two long yellow building bricks and sat driving them gently and pointlessly at one another.

Ms Simon – she pronounced it 'Simone' – was wearing what looked like a very deluxe poncho; some kind of violet cashmere. Her hair was in a pixie cut, her eyeshadow was a sheeny, pale-pink champagne, her blush apricot. She looked like the thick-waisted but winsome model who would appear in a magazine next to the words FABULOUS AT ANY AGE.

'Mr Tomlinson, Dr Tomlinson, won't you come in,' she said, indicating two chairs upholstered in green felt. There was a salt lamp in the room.

'Are you expelling her?' I said. I saw no reason to put myself through niceties.

Ms Simon said, 'Would you like a liquorice tea?'

'I would like,' I began, 'for my son to graduate preschool without permanent spinal trauma.'

She smiled at Gaby, who was also in the room. 'Some tea, Gaby? Thank you so much.'

When the door closed she sighed a long luxurious sigh. I wondered if she was counting to four.

'Samuel is such a —'

There was a knock.

'Such a?' said Connor, his face hopeful. 'Such a what?'

I shot him a look that he didn't acknowledge. Ms Simon ignored him and called, 'Yes?'

Deidre was wearing a sombre pinafore, charcoal with red buttons at the shoulders, and black boots that looked like part of a wetsuit. The restrained palette must have been her way of acknowledging the gravity of the situation.

The discussion did not proceed smoothly. Deidre said the fall was an accident; I put it to her that her child was a sociopath. Ms Simon nodded gravely. Eventually, after we'd been circling each other for fifteen minutes, Ms Simon said, 'I think we should bring the children in.'

They entered with their usual attitudes: Samuel's wide-eyed trepidation, Luna's thuggish nonchalance.

Ms Simon put a twinkle in her eye when she addressed the children. I wanted to tell Samuel that it was a trap, that all charm is a trap, but it was too late – he was already mesmerised, sitting on one of the child-sized chairs that Gaby had added to the semicircle on our side of the desk, sticking as many knuckles in his mouth as he could fit.

'Now,' Ms Simon said, 'no-one here is in any trouble. All right? We just want you to tell us everything that happened. Samuel, why don't you go first?'

Something a cop would say. I wanted to tell Samuel not to say anything incriminating, or stupid. Connor put his hand on my thigh. I realised I had almost launched out of my seat.

Samuel kept his gaze on Ms Simon, locked on her, and I could see how she enjoyed this, could see the bullet point on her executive-level résumé: *Key Skill: excellence in establishing rapport.*

'Luna pushed me,' Samuel said. He said it all in a rush, like it escaped from him, like it pained him to admit it.

Ms Simon smiled.

Luna tried to interrupt. 'No I didn't!' she began. 'I didn't! I —'

Ms Simon's smile was calm and immovable. 'Luna, you'll have your turn in just a moment.' She turned back to Samuel. 'When did she push you?'

'I was waiting my turn for slide.'

'Were the two of you talking? Do you know why she pushed you?'

Tears appeared in his eyes. He shook his head. 'Don't know,' he said. 'Don't know.'

Then he started crying in earnest. It was embarrassing how openly he wailed. Connor was the one who went to him, helped him blow his nose – which he did with great zeal and limited accuracy – and made the requisite murmuring noises.

'Luna?' said Ms Simon. 'What do you remember?'

I almost smirked. It was impossible to prove a negative. Good luck, kid, I thought. It was only then, realising she wasn't answering the question, that I really focused on Luna's broad face. Her brows were tilted in confusion. Her cheeks were bright red. Her eyes were wet, though she didn't cry. She looked at her mother, and her terror was real.

I saw that she was telling the truth.

'I didn't,' she said, finally, her chest heaving with rapid breaths.

Wow, I thought. She really is a child. She seemed fragile, unformed; I suddenly sensed the weight of my advantage over her.

She started shaking her head. 'He's lying!' she said.

She even did a dramatic courtroom point at my sobbing son, who by now had saturated the shoulder of Connor's shirt with his various secretions.

Deidre weighed in.

'Ms Simon,' she said, adding a slight French accent to the name, as though this would buy her extra points for accuracy, for attention to detail. 'They're little kids. Who knows what happened? It's his word versus hers. I think we should just draw a line under this and move on.' She sat back, hands linked primly on her gut.

Ms Simon gave her a look filled with great concern. 'My worry is that this is becoming a pattern of behaviour with Luna,' she said, smiling when she said the child's name, as though Luna were a dog who would understand only that word and none of the others.

'What I propose, and what I hope all parties will agree is for the best, is that both children attend counselling; Samuel for his trauma, Luna for her tendency towards finding a physical outlet for her aggression. I suggest we also have Luna sign a behavioural contract, in which she promises never to touch another child without their consent. How does that sound?'

Her voice was like butter.

Luna started pulling on Deidre's pinafore. 'Mum, I didn't do it,' she said. 'I didn't!' She sounded desperate.

Deidre laid a comforting hand on the top of her child's head. 'I'm not sending her to counselling for something she didn't do,' she said, smiling, looking around, hoping to find support in the room. 'She's only three. There's been some confusion. That's all.'

'I understand this must be difficult,' said Ms Simon. 'However, while we cherish all our pupils at Blossomings, safety must be paramount. I'm afraid these are the conditions of Luna's return to learning. If they don't suit your needs, I will completely understand if you would like to enrol her elsewhere.'

Deidre took a moment to comb her fingers through Luna's beautiful strawberry-blonde hair. The child clung to her mother, staring at me, at Connor, at Samuel, with genuine fear and genuine hatred. The expression on her mother's face showed, in a less raw manner, that she felt the same way.

She swallowed and it was audible. 'I think I see what's happening here,' she said. Her voice was trembling. 'This little snake of a child' – here she looked at Samuel, who was still snivelling – 'has invented a story to get my daughter into trouble. He's gone so far as to throw himself off the equipment, and because you're so scared of a fucking lawsuit —'

'Language,' I said, not quite under my breath.

Deidre turned her shrewd gaze to me. 'Oh piss off,' she said. 'Do you think I don't know who you are? What you do? Do *you* know?' she said, addressing Ms Simon. 'This woman makes bombs. She literally makes fucking weapons that blow little kids like these sky-high.'

I wondered how she knew that. Was she obsessed with me? Had she been googling my name deep into the night, reading the corporate profile that popped up on Raleigh's website?

'Deidre, I am going to have to ask you to be mindful of your language,' said Ms Simon.

'Seriously?' Deidre spat. 'That's what you care about? Here we are because one child fell – deliberately, I might add – a few feet onto a safety mat. She's out there dreaming up ways to blow thousands of kids to kingdom come and you honestly don't give a shit?'

Connor chose this moment to speak. 'It's not like that,' he said, his voice firm. 'It's like karate.'

Ms Simon drew the meeting to a close.

We drove home in companionable silence. Samuel slept in the back seat. That night the domestic things happened in quiet harmony; Connor and I were gracious with each other, feeding and bathing Samuel, setting the table, pouring wine, stacking the dishwasher. In bed I felt the cool tip of Connor's enquiries at my hip; and though it didn't quite happen, it almost did.

It was a week or so later that I had the idea that Samuel would make an ideal donor for Connor. He had no parasites, no history of sexually transmitted diseases; he hadn't had time to develop a dependency on alcohol or drugs. Connor had read about DIY faecal transplants, but thought it was too risky. He wanted the doctor, the twilight anaesthetic, the certainty that the donation would be sprayed all the way up to the top of his bowels. I convinced him to try it my way.

I watched an instructional video and let Samuel watch it with me. In it, a man demonstrated how to make the solution, by putting a chocolate-coated banana into a blender with water and salt. I thought Samuel would be horrified at the sight of the banana, but he just watched, fixated, as the mixture whizzed to the consistency of a milkshake.

The next day, I explained to Samuel that he had to pass his stool into a sterile plastic container because his donation was very precious. This explanation was good enough for him; he nodded, sombre as a bishop. I let him stay in the kitchen while I made the solution and drew it into an enema bulb. Afterwards the blender went straight into the rubbish bin outside.

I didn't allow Samuel to watch the next part. I barely wanted to see it myself. Connor and I locked ourselves in the ensuite. I laid garbage bags on the floor and handed Connor a pillow that he could rest on while the enema took effect. I wore gloves and a mask, and I tried to be gentle as I parted my husband's buttocks and saw the thick, pasted down whorls of hair in there, and the aperture at their centre.

'It's all right,' Connor said, when he thought I wasn't applying sufficient pressure. 'It doesn't hurt.'

I prodded harder; then I squeezed as hard as I could. When the bulb was empty I sat with him for the requisite time stipulated by the websites. Connor lay on the pillow, naked and groaning. When the timer went off I left the room so that he could evacuate his bowels in private.

'What do you think?' I asked when he emerged, still unsteady, from the shower. 'Do you think it worked?'

His smile was like weak tea. 'I feel better already,' he said.

Samuel was glad to hear how much he'd helped. I never asked him about Luna again; I didn't need to. She undertook the counselling and returned to Blossomings, and if she was seething with anger, anger that would last the rest of her miserable life, that wasn't my problem.

Besides, there was nothing to ask. I already knew the truth. I knew what I'd seen in Luna's face. But I was not appalled at my son. I'd go for walks with him and Connor, and watch him surrounded by cranky, grasping gulls. I'd watch how he tempted them with a soggy chip and then chased them all away, giving them nothing. In a moment they'd come back, gathering around him, their eyes on the morsel he held. Their violence, their displeasure, was all directed at one another.

The game delighted him. He smiled at me and I smiled back, finally feeling it, that glow of love I was supposed to have for my own flesh and blood.

Ah, my little starling. He wouldn't be the kind of person who seemed particularly talented, or beautiful, or charming, or forceful. He might not leave much of an impression at all. But when the time came – and it always came, always – he would be the one to push the button.

Blood Bag

It was like pouring out bottle after bottle of expensive wine. Only it came out of bags rather than bottles. And it was thicker, more viscous. And only on occasion did I let it touch my tongue.

O-negative, A-positive, even AB, the rare stuff. I used it all.

It worked, too. Every evening I would go into my garden and feel a deep, thrumming satisfaction as I noted the progress of my vegetables. I rubbed the goblinish skin of the pumpkins, watched each aubergine nose its way out of the calyx until eventually it hung, glossy, pendulous as a testicle. The zucchinis were smug and fat among the undergrowth.

I'd found the job at the donation centre in the early days of being alone. It soothed me, the sight of all those bags of blood chilled down to lizard temperatures in the refrigerator.

My ex-husband was a doctor. I had been a nurse. I remember my husband's clever hands stretching out the thick beige pantyhose that had been part of my uniform. He was fascinated by them, their grip and give, the way they clung to my calves and thighs.

'You're like a snake,' he'd say, picking up a pair from the floor. 'Leaving your skins everywhere.'

I loved my vegetables. To me, love meant sitting in my garden until darkness fell, waiting for the slugs to make their approach. I read somewhere that the bottom of a slug is one giant foot, making rhythmic contractions to propel the animal forward. This disgusted me; their slick secretions reflecting silver in the moonlight disgusted me. I felt no pity when I poured salt down their backs.

Some people say that salt will dissolve a slug, but this is incorrect. It pulls the blood from them – if you can call it blood, that greenish-coppery fluid that fizzes into a pool around their shrinking bodies. The salt works by osmosis: the process by which liquid moves from a weaker solution to a stronger one.

I took precautions, of course. I was suspicious of my colleagues, of my neighbours. I was careful when I slipped the bags into my purse. When I arrived home from the centre each evening, I transferred their contents to a watering can before I went outside.

And I was right to be suspicious. My neighbours couldn't help themselves, peering over the fence. 'Rosie, what are you putting on those pumpkins? Rosie, that aubergine – what a monster!' I would nod in agreement, stroking the dark surface of the thing, so shiny it seemed wet. I stroked until it squeaked.

Sometimes I thought about the donors: cheerful, civic-minded people. They liked to admire the dot of blood on the cotton wool taped to the inside of their elbows. These were the kinds of people who wore stickers: 'I gave'. *I gave.* What a laugh.

I didn't give.

Who had ever given anything to me?

One beautiful spring evening, just before he left, my husband looked at the balding lawn and vacant flowerbeds. He said, 'We'll never grow anything here.'

I'm well aware that there are more humane ways to dispatch slugs. You can let them drown happily in beer. You can kill them instantly by dropping them into boiling water. But the dried-out, green-white rings around my garden pleased me. I thought they might act as a deterrent to other pests.

All my watering cans tend to rust through quickly. I keep the ruined ones. I like to line them up against the wall of the house and admire the rust-rimmed gashes in their sides.

I'm mostly iron now, I think. I close my eyes and scan my body for evidence: trying to sense my magnetic field, or imagine the efficiency with which oxygen is delivered to my various systems. I hold still and listen to my hurrying blood: in a rush to burn holes through the vessel that carries it.

The Drydown

Have you noticed any changes? Good or bad?

I don't cry so often. That, and my digestion's better.

Better? You mean, more regular?

Yes.

Anything else? Have there been side effects? Nausea? Sweating? Problems achieving climax?

The doctor's pen was expensive; gloss-black, heavy. It scratched away, competent and discreet, making remarks that he could review later, at his leisure.

No, I said. Then I thought about it, and added, It makes it easier to give things away.

Andrew had suggested we move in together. This is how I know that it's not so hard to give things away. He came to the apartment I was sharing with my sister, Isolde, and after letting his gaze range over the living room, with its balding velvet sofa and worn clothes and used teacups strewn around the floor, told me to lay out my things and assign each of them a score from one to ten, based on its usefulness. We took everything that scored below a nine to the charity shop, the nearby Greek Orthodox one that reeks of mothballs, where most clothes are hung up so high that the tiny, black-clad women who work there have to retrieve them with a hook attached to a pole. They have my formal dress now, and my childhood toys. They have my mother's gloves. Too small for you, said Andrew, and he was right; they wouldn't stretch further than my knuckles.

And my grandmother's wedding dress – they have that too. Andrew pointed out that I'll never wear it. For example, he said, if we were getting married, you'd want something simpler, more modern. And if you're not going to wear it, why keep it?

Andrew was in favour of them. The SNRIs. Of course I love you, he said. It's just, all the crying. The moods. I can't handle you when you're like that.

Everyone was in favour of the SNRIs, though. Everyone but Isolde. She's like our mother was: too thin and proud of it, tall, chainsmoking, glamorous. She's a fashion photographer. She said – it's not an illness, Luce. Crying. Screaming. Being a smart-arse. Saying no for no good reason. It's called a personality.

I don't see Isolde very often now. Last time Andrew and I had dinner with her, she told him he dressed like the kind of man who hangs around primary schools. Later, when Andrew asked about her superannuation, Isolde said nothing, just popped her knuckles one by one.

When we were children, Isolde and I used to fight over my grandmother's wedding dress. Whoever wore it was the queen; the other had to play a variety of roles: dog, princess, king, jester, knight. The dress came into my possession because the other thing we fought over, my mother's engagement ring with the central diamond missing, belongs to Isolde now. She wears it on a chain around her neck.

In your brain – this is how the doctor had put it to me – when something happens to make you feel good, you release a chemical. It's released by one neuron – he drew a circle – travels along the synapse – he added a curved line – and is absorbed back into another neuron, like this. He made a gesture, a bird's talons closing around its prey. The Serotonin and Norepinephrine Reuptake Inhibitors, he said, prevent a neuron taking the serotonin back, so it stays circulating in your brain. See?

And that will make me happy? I asked.

No, not happy, not exactly, he said. It will even you out.

How often, now, when I'm at work, do I think of this phrase. I am evened out as I giftwrap the gold and cream and black embossed boxes. I am evened out helping men choose how their girlfriend or mistress or wife should smell. I am evened out when I talk to women about the idea of a signature scent, the one perfume that will help them be remembered.

It was my mother who taught me about perfume, about the families into which fragrances arrange themselves: floral and chypre, woody and oriental; she taught me about vetiver and tuberose, oakmoss and tobacco, orange blossom, rose, violet, aldehydes, musk. She once did what I do now, except that she worked in a small boutique whose owners were French, and who taught her how to complain about customers in a language they wouldn't understand. When Isolde and I were little, she taught us the words they used to say: *Salope. Putain. Connard.* And when a customer left without buying anything: *Va te faire foutre*, whispered under the breath.

I worry that while I'm on the SNRIs my senses will be dulled. The doctor said, No, you might be a little less sensitive, emotionally, but it won't affect your physical senses, not at all. But I doubt him. I breathe in the new scents that arrive, and the check-lists that used to form in my head – rain, crushed stems, lilacs, peonies, sweet pea, jasmine – just stop, like a road at the edge of a cliff. They evade me now, those other notes; the faint, crucial ones separating one scent from another, which I used to be able to catch.

The one thing I will not throw out, despite the SNRIs, is what Andrew calls my 'old ladies', my collection of original perfumes – Shocking, Mitsouko, Shalimar, Fracas. There are modern versions, but they aren't the same. Too many of the original ingredients have been banned because they're toxic, or were scraped from the anal glands of some endangered animal. And most people don't like them, anyway. Too strong, too much. Overpowering. Andrew sniffed the stopper of one, said it was enough to wake the dead, washed his hands, and then all afternoon kept smelling his fingers, saying, How do you stand it? The smell? It never goes away.

That's called the drydown, I told him. There's the initial burst, the top notes, then the heart notes, and then the base notes – the drydown. And if it lasts and lasts and won't disappear, even after a shower, well, that's a good thing.

He shook his head. Said, Fine, keep them if you must.

I lined them up on the dressing table. The next day, he moved them to the cabinet of the guest bathroom.

I thought you couldn't bear to touch them, I said.

I wore rubber gloves, was his reply.

He never smells them on me, anyway. I am almost always wearing something I have to wear for work. What's that? Andrew will ask some days, when he picks me up in his sleek sedan. It's nice, he'll say. Sweet. Feminine. Pleasant.

Recently he made his special dish, whiting with a white wine and parsley sauce. He set an LED candle in the middle of the table. My gut didn't sink, the way it would have, once. It just rolled a little, like when you step into an elevator that travels more quickly than you were expecting. He talked about work, about the golf game he had planned for the weekend, about the holiday we would take in June, about the discount he got at the resort.

Then: Do you ever think about marriage?

My mind blanked, a train entering a tunnel.

Sometimes, I said.

I want to know if it's something you would want, he said.

Are you —

I'm not asking, if that's what you mean. I don't think the time is right. Not yet. But I want to know what you would say. If I did ask.

I pared flesh off the bones of my fish.

Well? Would you accept?

I looked up.

Yes, I said. I think I would.

It's Isolde, on the phone.

Luce, I need a favour. It's for a shoot.

I'm on my lunchbreak, eating a salad. Andrew says I need to reduce the amount of refined carbohydrates in my diet. He says they cause inflammation.

Okay. I say. What is it?

Nanna's dress. Her wedding dress. We'll look after it, I swear. It's for a nouveau-Edwardian thing we're doing. It'll be perfect, gorgeous. I'll even get it dry-cleaned afterwards.

I can't say anything. A piece of lettuce, on my fork, is suspended in the air. It is good to know that some feelings are still strong enough to reach the surface, to break through the synapse-waltz of the SNRIs.

I don't have it, I say finally.

What do you mean?

I gave it away. When I moved. I didn't think I'd ever use it, so …

There is a pause.

So you just decided. Just like that?

It's just a dress.

Where did you take it, Lucetta? Where exactly did it go?

I tell her. She hangs up.

Strange: once, after an exchange like this, I would have felt anxious. I would have played the scene over and over in my head, imagining what I could have said differently, done differently; I would have wondered whether to call back. This time, I finish my salad, wash my hands, and go back to work.

The new perfume we're promoting is called Dream Haze. It's aimed at females aged fourteen to twenty-two. The bottles are lurid pink, studded with false diamonds. I inhale my wrist and list the ingredients, trying to distinguish individual notes in the vaguely familiar fruity cloud: lychee, pink pepper, apple. It feels like a sugar high. My head spins. We sell Dream Haze consistently all day, to teenagers with their mothers, teenagers alone paying with their fast-food wages, and occasionally to older women in suits with nails long enough to tap against the counter.

Down through the afternoon the smell of Dream Haze morphs, from the initial burst of sweetness, like a piñata exploding, to a languorous, hot-afternoon, tropical-fruit heart. Then, as it enters the drydown, base notes that are all synthetic: peach, watermelon, vanilla. Residual sugar. Sticky fingers.

Andrew picks me up when I finish work. A shock from the car door, then the smell of leather.

He says, after a minute, What is that? You smell wonderful.

At a red light, he leans over and breathes in.

It's gorgeous. Really.

Not too sweet?

No, he said. It's perfect. What's it called?

Then I remember what Dream Haze reminds me of more than anything. It's the air fresheners in our house, the little vials plugged into the wall that release a puff of Aqua Breeze or Exotic Sunset as you walk past.

When we arrive home, there's a box outside the door. Andrew picks it up, looks at the note, sees that I am looking over his shoulder, passes the box to me.

The note reads:

Va te faire foutre.
xx

What is it? Andrew asks.

I don't know, I say.

I wait until I can hear him moving around downstairs. I untie the string. Inside, I see my grandmother's dress, a mohair sweater that belonged to our mother, a plush toy horse I owned as a child.

I sink my face into the box. What I can smell: mothballs, dust, mildew, dry-cleaning fluid, wet sheep, talcum powder. And old, dried sweat.

And there is something else in there, too, some other note. I try to place it, but it's like seeing a person from behind, someone you're not sure you know. It slips away.

I hide the box inside another box. I go downstairs to Andrew, and put my arms around his waist and my face against his back.

But now, whenever I'm alone in the house, I slip the box out and inhale its contents. I can't name it, not yet, that last, elusive part of the scent. But I know it. I know that I know it. And I know it will be there, waiting for me; I know it is strong enough to last.

Rip

The success or failure of a dive is decided as soon as your weight leaves the platform. Two things are determined in that fraction of a second: how high you'll reach, and the angle at which you'll drop. Once you're committed, that's it. Any mistake is impossible to correct.

For a dive from the ten-metre platform you have about one-and-a-half seconds to twist and flip your body in the way you've claimed you can. More height means more time, and time is everything when you're plummeting towards the water at terminal speed.

When I was a diver, we spent a lot of time at training working on our takeoffs. I remember the burn in my calves, the twin bulbs of the gastrocnemius firing together to propel me upwards, over and over. I remember how my wrists used to ache. I remember the pre-training ritual: my whole team taping up our less stable joints, bracing ourselves as well as we could for impact.

Our coach, Aleks, would make us drill our dives until we were through pain and into numbness. I suppose that's why I saw my takeoffs improve under his instruction. I mean this literally. I saw it because the assistant coach – his wife, Julie – filmed all our sessions. Every week he'd make us watch them back and tell him where we could make adjustments; tell him if our knees were too bent, our spines too rigid, if our gazes weren't focused where they should be focused. Julie said very little during these reviews. She'd stand there with her finger hovering over the rewind button, anticipating his next request.

'I want you jumping in your dreams,' Aleks used to say.

I don't remember dreaming about my takeoffs. But I always woke up sore.

I was born with an ideal diver's body. That's not bragging. It's a body that's disproportionate: big-shouldered, flat-backed and flat-breasted, with no waist to speak of and short, thick legs.

'Thank God you've got a pretty face,' Lou would say when we went shopping. 'Thank God for that blonde hair.'

It was Lou who paid for the private girls' school where I was first spotted as a potential diver. They had a team which would funnel its best performers into elite squads, bound for national and international competition. The school had its own diving pool, in a hot and humid glass-walled room where the oak-veneer benches were always slick with condensation.

I had no interest in sports, but everyone was obligated to participate in the school's swimming carnival. I came a lazy sixth in my year's 200-metre freestyle event, and was peeling my swimming cap from my head, feeling the pull at the roots of my hair, when the diving coach approached me.

Her name was Miss Tyrell. She was a small woman, but not in a petite or delicate way. She was small in the manner of a shrunken head, wizened, with sunken eyes that she outlined in kohl. She wore incongruous bright scrunchies: orange, green, magenta.

The kohl eyes sized up my figure. 'I think you should try diving,' she said.

When I declined, she called Lou.

'The woman was pretty adamant,' Lou said one night, rummaging through a box of noodles with her chopsticks, looking for any bits of charred meat she'd missed. 'She said there are people out there who get surgery to have a physique like yours. Something about their vertebrae.'

'Why would anyone want my vertebrae?'

'Fucked if I know.' Lou found a piece of pork and ate it.

'I'm not doing it,' I said.

'Not so fast. There's one other thing she brought up,' said Lou, peering at me over her glasses. 'The incident.'

I rolled my eyes. I didn't want to talk about The Incident. To my mind, I hadn't done anything wrong, not really. It had only been a joke. It was during a school play, a production of *The Crucible*. Everyone in my drama class had to take on a role in the cast or crew. I'd volunteered to be costume assistant, the job I thought would require the least amount of commitment.

The girl who played Goody Proctor was a serious type with ambitions of becoming a Shakespearean actor. She spent her lunchtimes pacing back and forth memorising monologues, and had dandruff all along her centre part, like snow scraped to the sides of a road. During the production, she treated me like I was her personal attendant. She'd do breathing exercises with her eyes closed while I buttoned her into her gown. While I helped her into the black boots she wore on stage, she'd put a hand on my head and lean her weight onto my skull. 'My apron isn't steamed!' she said to me once, in a panicked voice, and when I said no-one would care she threw it on the floor – not being quite brave enough, I think, to throw it at me.

All things considered, what I did wasn't that bad. During a scene change I started pulling a dress down over her head, and then on impulse pulled it back towards myself, twisting it so the dark wool covered her face. I remember her stark, denuded body, her thin arms with their visible network of blue veins. They waved around, grappled at her throat, then grasped at the empty air. One breast flopped out of her bra.

It was just a prank, over in seconds. And I wasn't the only one who laughed; the other girls in their gowns and glued-on beards had seen how funny it was. She'd looked so comic, so clumsy, lurching around in her panic.

But someone told, and the school didn't look kindly on The Incident. My record there was hardly pristine, and the only reason I wasn't expelled was that Lou went down to the school and stayed for hours, negotiating my punishment down to a suspension, a probation, and a letter of apology, which Lou wrote for me.

I am so deeply ashamed ... she wrote.

'But I'm not ashamed,' I said, looking over her shoulder at the computer.

'You're telling me,' she replied. She reached back and absently patted me on the cheek. I watched the cursor flash. The words *This experience will make me a better person* appeared on the screen.

It would be wise, Lou told me now, to accept the school's invitation to participate in the diving squad. So I agreed. I wasn't expecting to show aptitude, but my advantages soon made themselves felt. I mastered each of the simple dives we learned to take, first from the three-metre then the five-metre springboard. I could somersault, and then double-somersault; my twists were tighter than those of my teammates, my entries into the water more precise.

We competed against other schools. Soon there was a clattering array of base-metal medals hanging from the knob of my bedroom door.

I enjoyed this newly discovered talent, not so much for its own sake as for the responses it elicited from others. 'I wish I could do that,' a girl would say to me after I hauled my weight from the pool. And I'd think, I bet you do. Or, Good luck with that. Or, Too bad.

In certain moods, I'd encourage the younger girls on the team to emulate me. 'You can do it,' I'd say, knowing I'd be able to watch their failure from the sidelines as I squeezed the water out of my hair.

'Don't you dare,' Miss Tyrrell would say to them, arms folded.

One day, one of the youngest girls, brave and grinning, went against Miss Tyrell's directives and copied my dive. To my surprise, and hers, she succeeded. She emerged from the water ecstatic.

'Did you see? Did you?' she said, running to me when she got out of the pool.

Miss Tyrell's kohl eyes narrowed to glinting specks in her face. 'I hope I don't have to remind you who's in charge of this team,' she said.

'Whatever.'

'Excuse me?'

'Whatever,' I repeated slowly, sounding out the syllables.

There was a moment of stillness before Miss Tyrell lost her temper. While she yelled I tried to recall The Incident, and all Lou's efforts to keep me at the school; I tried to weather the torrent of rage without responding. For several excruciating seconds I examined my stumpy fingernails, chewed into raggedness. But then she said, 'Who do you think you are, anyway?' with such a curdled, sour note in her voice that I looked up. Everything receded except her lined face, the wet slivers of her eyes.

I called her names, a whole long various parade of them: whore, bitch, cunt, even words I'd never usually think to say – cow, slag, witch. When I ran out of insults I started in about the scrunchies. I remember that she just let me talk until I had exhausted my repertoire. And then, her own rage seemingly spent, she said calmly, 'Joan, it's such a shame that a talent like yours has been wasted on a person like you.'

I went home and told Lou.

'She said that? That fucking moll. Don't worry, I'll go down there. Raise some hell,' Lou said.

She'd taken off her shirt to eat a kebab over the sink. Her bra had sweat stains in the middle, dried with salt like a tide line.

'No, don't.'

'You sure?'

'I'm sure.'

She went anyway.

I finished school without distinction, and spent the following summer doing nothing, looking forward to nothing. Diving was over, or so I thought, and I felt no urgency to study, to work, to make a name or a future for myself. It seemed to me that everyone I knew had such small ambitions, enrolling in courses in accounting, or web design, or osteopathy.

Meanwhile, I ate ice cream and dreamed of an amorphous kind of glory. Most of this dreaming occurred at the local swimming pool, a great swarming expanse where people's towels marked their territory.

I was spending most summer days there with girls I called my friends. Sometimes we swam, but we spent most of our time coolly assessing each day's assortment of boys. We surveyed boys we'd seen around our neighbourhood, boys we knew from parties and formals, boys who had taken the bus from shabbier suburbs than ours. We could see who had a spray of violent acne across the shoulder blades, who had an unattractive, chimpish gathering of dark hair at the base of his spine, who was so thin that the back of his navel popped through the front like a prolapse.

Behind the main pool there was a ten-metre diving platform. It loomed above its own separate pool, the water of which was weirdly green. It was rare to see someone dive from that tower. When it happened, it was usually those same boys, some squeamish and cringing, some only too happy to go sprinting down the platform and fling themselves off the end, their limbs wheeling in helpless fury before they hit the water and sent waves slopping over the sides of the pool.

One day a pudgy boy in hibiscus-print boardshorts sauntered over to us, dripping.

'Did you see that, ladies?' he said, the giddiness from his first act of bravery goading him into another.

A friend, a girl whose most memorable attribute was her ability to open bottles with her eye socket, inclined her head in my direction. 'She's a diver,' she said. 'A real one. Dipshit.'

He looked at me, unimpressed. 'Prove it,' he said.

I didn't have to accept his invitation. But I found myself walking to the tower. Yes, I'd been a diver, but our school only had a five-metre platform. The ten-metre was a vastly different thing. The ladder was dull, dark iron and so hot it burned my hands and the soles of my feet. Once I was at the top I remember shivering – big, involuntary, full-body shivers – despite the heat. There were palm trees whose fronds skittered in the wind. There was green mildew on the wide platform, and tiny winking fragments of quartz throughout the concrete. They prickled my arches as I walked to the edge. I looked down to the green water.

I knew that hesitation would only make the fear worse, so I did what I'd seen those boys do – I retreated to the back of the platform, then took a running jump off the end.

The dive was not an elegant thing. I probably shouldn't have attempted a double somersault. In fact, what I did was called a smack, which is exactly what it sounds like. I smacked the whole back of my body on the water, because I had overreached, overbalanced, and couldn't correct. I'd let lapse the skills that would allow me to pull myself into a vertical, self-preserving line. By the time I realised this, it was too late.

But the length of the drop was exhilarating; I heard my own gasp in my ears. And the feeling when I hit the water was like nothing else. It hurt at first; it was a shock. There was a moment of total disorientation, when things went dark and cold and quiet. Nothing existed except me and the deep water, now seething with fine, moussey bubbles.

After a moment that water returned me to the surface, unharmed, intact. I'd never been so serene, even though my head rang, even though my skin was stinging.

At home that night, Lou came into my room while I was getting undressed. She never knocked. I spun and said, 'Hey!' my hands covering my chest.

'What the fuck is that?' she said.

I twisted my head so I could see myself in the mirrored panels of the wardrobe. I'd hit the water so hard that it had left a broad white blot on my back. The blot was the shape of the water as I collided with it, the shape of the splash I was in the process of making.

'Sunburn,' I said.

'Bullshit,' said Lou.

I don't know why I lied. But I also didn't tell her about the man who'd come up to me as my friends and I were leaving the pool.

'Nice smack,' he said.

My friends, a few paces away, turned back to openly ogle this man, who was old enough to be interesting and not old enough to be disgusting. He had grey-streaked hair combed back from his face, thick-rimmed black glasses, stubble on his jaw and down his neck. His muscles were solid, not the stringy, twitchy muscles of a boy. Even his gut looked hard, like a gorilla's. And he wore the cleanest white T-shirt I'd ever seen. I lived in a house of persistent stains: white, flaky deodorant stains, brown fake-tan stains, peach and pink makeup smears. His T-shirt was so clean it dazzled me.

'Thanks.'

'Are you a diver?'

'Not exactly.'

'But that wasn't your first time, was it?'

'No.' I paused. 'I'm … retired.'

He laughed. I narrowed my eyes against the glare of the sun.

'Well,' he said. 'Here – let me know if I can talk you out of retirement.'

He gave me his card. It was thin and white with a logo, and in blocky black capitals: ALEKS KORSAK, COACH. He told me he worked at a diving club in an outer suburb, a club which, he assured me, was well respected in diving circles. He mentioned a series of names, people he'd coached who had gone on to achieve impressive things. I didn't recognise any of them.

I slid the card into my wallet, behind the loyalty cards and the debit card Lou watched like a hawk.

'Who was that?' one of my friends asked when he was gone.

'Some pervert, I guess,' I said.

For days afterwards, I felt a burn in the centre of my back. The smack felt as though it produced its own heat, low and constant, radiating outwards from my body.

It doesn't seem right to say that Lou is my sister. She's almost forty. Our mother died when Lou was twenty and I had just turned one. She fought like hell to keep me, and she likes to remind me of this fact every time we fight, which is often, and furiously.

We have money now, but we didn't for a long time. We've never gotten used to it. We have nice plates but eat off paper ones, the way we used to when she was in law school. We can afford to shop at the little organic grocer, but still go to the grotty supermarket two suburbs away. In the deli section, Lou pretends she can speak Italian to the unimpressed woman in a navy apron and hairnet who's been there as long as we can remember. Once, Lou pointed to a piece of cheese. The woman picked it up and asked Lou a question in Italian. Lou, smiling, said, *'Sì!'* and we watched as the woman fed the cheese into a machine that pulverised it into a pale powder. She slapped a barcode on it and held Lou's gaze.

'Grazie,' Lou said.

Now Lou buys the beautiful things she always wanted: designer clothes, expensive lipsticks, handbags, sunglasses. She wears needly stilettos every day. Her bunions are unbelievable.

But her beautiful things all end up ruined in one way or another; the lipstick mashed all through her bag in a bloody, waxy, high-pigment mess, a pen exploding in a beautiful suit jacket, pair after pair of sunglasses sat on or stood on or lost. Her collection of expensive heels lies, a black and tan jumble, on the floor of her room.

Lou is a criminal defence barrister. Her cases have never shocked me because I grew up with her telling me about them. A man caught sending explicit emails to a thirteen-year-old. A man who worked in a women's clothing shop and installed hidden cameras in the change-rooms. A man who had been an anaesthetist, who touched women when they were unconscious.

When I was a child, Lou tried to use the law to frighten me. For example: I had a habit of thievery. One day I filled my pockets with chocolate bars while Lou stuffed the trolley with Lean Cuisine and Rice Bubbles.

When she realised what I'd done, she didn't make me take them back. We ate them together. Behind us, on the mute TV, cartoons went on in their manic way, flashing and racing in ugly primary colours.

'I need to explain something to you,' she said, flaying the wrapper from a bar of chocolate. 'I'm studying to be a lawyer. Do you know what that means?'

I nodded. I knew this one. 'You put people in jail.'

'Exactly,' Lou said. She hadn't specialised in pervs yet, on keeping them out instead of putting them in.

'And if you steal things – that means, you take something without paying for it first, or you take something that's not yours – you could go to jail.'

My heart sickened at this. 'Will I go to jail?'

'Not this time,' Lou said. 'But next time you might not be so lucky. Do you know what happens in jail?'

I shook my head, my eyes fixed on the way her features all drew together towards the centre of her face.

'You go to the electric chair.'

She went on to explain that this was a chair that would fry me to death, fry me until I crumbled like a piece of burned toast. My eyeballs would explode.

'So next time you're going to steal something,' Lou said, 'be very, very careful.'

Lou was in the middle of a trial when I called the number on the card. I was glad; these were the times I was most invisible to her. Lou always got anxious during trials, often too anxious to eat. To offset this, in the weeks before one commenced she'd force-feed herself junk food. She went for whatever was most dense with calories: boxes of doughnuts leaving their snow of powdered sugar over her documents, Nutella eaten straight from the jar. KFC was a perennial favourite. She liked the colonel's face, she said. It was a face you could trust.

Lou's anxiety also made her sweat. To combat this, she would buy a pharmacy-strength deodorant and roll it all over her body every morning. I'd come into the living room and she'd be sitting on the couch, papers strewn across the coffee table, rolling deodorant on the soles of her feet.

'I don't think you're supposed to put that everywhere,' I'd say, watching her take the deodorant that had just been on her feet and drag it around her hairline.

'I know what I'm doing,' she'd reply.

At night during trials, Lou would come home and start drinking – not wine, or even beer, but Midori, or Baileys – and continue until most of the bottle was gone. She unscrewed the smoke detector and smoked indoors. She slept in her clothes.

She didn't have any attention to spare for me. Her radar was elsewhere. And for this call, and for what might follow, I wanted privacy, to have space between me and her shrewdness, her indignation when she sensed I was keeping any kind of secret.

I called in the middle of the day; there was nowhere I needed to be. To fill my time now that school was over, Lou had badgered one of the barristers at her chambers into giving me a part-time job, which mostly involved either photocopying documents or shredding them. But other than the desultory ten hours a week I spent watching the green bar of light in the photocopier move back and forth, or the shredder turn evidence into noodles, my time during business hours was my own. I was safely alone, but I put the chain on the front door just in case.

To my surprise, a woman answered.

'Oh,' I said. 'I'm sorry, I must have the wrong number.'

'Who did you want?'

I stared at his name on the card, already foxed at the edges from all the handling I'd given it.

'Aleks Korsak,' I said, getting a weird squeeze of pleasure from saying his name.

'One moment,' she said.

She put me on hold. I didn't know it then, but the woman I was speaking to was Julie Korsak, Aleks's wife. She was the team's assistant coach, though I was never really sure whether this position was official. She also seemed to operate as the team manager, as Aleks's secretary, as an ersatz nurse for the girls on the team. It would be wrong to say she was always at his side; she was more like a satellite, orbiting him, surveying him from a distance and recording everything she saw.

The hold music was strange – an echoing piano felted with static. Later, whenever I heard this music I would imagine a tiny Julie Korsak inside the telephone, or suspended between telephones, mournfully playing the same tune over and over.

'Joan?' Aleks's voice cut through the music.

He invited me to observe a training session. 'Come over,' he said, and gave me the address. 'Have a look. See how you like it.'

I took a train and a bus to reach the aquatic centre. It was as grimy as I had expected. The building was yellow brick, the path leading up to it cracked and uneven. The plants surrounding the building were dun-coloured and drought-resistant.

I would not be joining an elite squad, that much was plain. This was only confirmed by the tour that Julie Korsak gave me, which took in the dirty grout in the showers, and a bandaid riding the ripples on the surface of the pool.

When I first walked in and Julie came up to me, I'd had the thought that her head was an odd shape, too oblong, like a carton of milk. Nevertheless I smiled, and she smiled, clutching my hand in both of hers.

'Hello, you must be Joan,' she said, pumping my hand. 'Welcome. It's so nice to meet you!' Then she fell silent, as though she'd used up her burst of geniality and had no idea what to say next. When she turned away, I saw that her jacket had *SQUAD* written in iron-on white letters on the back, to which she'd glued little pink and blue crystals.

The tour complete, I was invited to sit and watch the team train.

After welcoming me once more, Julie pulled out her phone, directed it at the platform, and started to record.

I saw my potential teammates line up at the back of the ten-metre platform and down its steps; I watched them drop off its edge. Some were more competent than others, but none were brilliant. Breathe, leap, splash – too slow, too weak, too timid. As rivals, I dismissed them one by one. When I grew bored of looking at them, I stared at Aleks, at his hair, at the place where it became stubble at the back of his neck. At the dip in the base of his spine. At his forearms. He paced, consulting a clipboard. The clean T-shirt was grey that day. He didn't seem to notice me at all.

He'd been a diver once. He'd told me as much. But he was never going to make it, I could see that; there was too much wrong with his body. He was too tall, for a start. Male divers shouldn't be taller than five-eight or -nine, and Aleks cleared six feet. It was his legs that were the problem. Anyone else would want those legs: long and trim. He looked good in shorts. But for diving you want a short lower body. You want legs that don't take too long to extend.

At the end of the session, after they'd changed, the girls assembled in a room near the pool, where a table, chairs, a whiteboard and a TV were set up. Aleks briskly introduced me to the team, who stared at me curiously. I found myself seated between Grace, who was round-faced and freckled, and Camilla, a long-necked, knock-kneed girl whose long dark hair was coiled on top of her head. Camilla's car keys were sprawled on the table; the photo ID attached to them indicated she was a student at the university Lou had attended – the one she'd wanted me to attend.

Julie Korsak plugged her phone into the TV and stood there dutifully selecting and playing videos of each dive. After a while,

Grace, who had been absent-mindedly taking pumps from a jumbo bottle of sorbolene and rubbing them into her biceps and calves, leaned over and said, 'So you got scouted?' There was a note of amusement in her voice. 'You must be pretty good.'

Before I could reply, Aleks spoke. 'Camilla?'

Camilla had pulled her jacket's sleeves down over her hands. 'Yes?'

'What am I looking at here?'

'My 204C.'

It was a back group dive: two somersaults in the tuck position.

'Yes. And?'

Camilla, prettily and glassily green-eyed, looked at him for a moment, saying nothing. She clasped her keys in one hand, as though she was going to pick them up and leave the room. After a moment I saw not her face, but her ears turn a bright, raw pink.

Aleks instructed his wife to replay the dive.

'Anything?'

Camilla was rigid, but shook her head. 'Sorry, I just —'

'No problem,' said Aleks calmly. 'We'll just watch it again.'

We watched it again, and again, and again, until even I felt a wave of nausea. The room had fallen into a thick, attentive quiet. Camilla's eyes looked wet.

Another of the girls said, 'Aleks, hey, can I go? I've got —'

His look silenced her. 'We can all go,' he said, 'once Camilla has identified her error. Come on, it's not that hard. It's something you've done dozens of times. Hundreds, probably. Well?' he said.

Camilla scratched her neck, and I heard the scratching, imagined the scraped-off cells collecting under her fingernails.

'She's diving blind,' I blurted out.

You're supposed to keep your eyes open when you dive. It's so you can find visual cues and orient yourself as you fall. Diving blind – that is, with your eyes shut – is a common mistake.

Everyone turned to look at me. Grace gave a minute shake of her head. *Shut up*, she was saying. *Shut up*.

I wondered if I'd be asked to leave. Camilla gave me a look that may have been relief or may have been loathing.

Aleks gave a curt nod. 'Thank you, Joan,' he said, 'for putting us out of our misery.'

As we were walking out, Grace said to me, 'He's kind of a prick. But she always does that.'

'Dives blind?'

'Plays dumb.'

'Oh.'

We'd fallen behind the others. We took a few more steps in silence before Grace said, 'They're fucking, you know.'

'What?'

She smiled. Her skin shone from the sorbolene. 'You heard me,' she said.

In the training sessions that followed, I wondered about the truth of Grace's claim. I watched Aleks and Camilla carefully, but there was nothing in the way he treated her that suggested any tender feeling. In fact, there were times when he seemed disgusted with her, shaking his head, turning his back. Even when she started to keep her eyes open, improving her overall execution as a result, he still managed to exude contempt.

Soon enough, I was able to experience his lack of mercy for myself. It turned out that this was the quality I liked best about him. I liked the way he barked '*Now*' when he wanted me to come out of a dive. I liked how he would approach me while

I was on the lat pull-down machine and push his fingers hard into the centre of my spine, not letting me release until I had pulled the bar all the way into my sternum. I liked that when he was impressed he didn't say so, just betrayed it through a surprised flick of both eyebrows.

When I failed in front of Aleks, smacking, coming out too late or early, missing my cues, I burned with shame. He never laughed it off, never reassured me. He would just peer down his nose as I dragged myself out of the pool, a stony look on his face.

With his foot in my back my pike got tighter; with his bark in my ears I learned to time my verticals. His was a mediocre team, that was obvious, but he was a good coach. A search revealed he had also been a good diver; if his figure had been proportioned more kindly, he might have been a brilliant one.

'Does this hurt?' he'd ask, kneeling above me on one of the blue vinyl mats in the weights room, pushing my knee into my chest until I was sure that something would give, something would rupture.

'No.'

'How about now?

'No.'

'Now?'

I'd force myself to smile. 'I can't feel a thing.'

He'd laugh. He knew what he was doing.

And meanwhile, there was Julie, standing back, catching every error, every mistimed jump, every failure to complete, every smack, on her phone. We weren't allowed the luxury of new beginnings. We were never allowed to forget.

Lou had been glad to hear I'd resumed diving, and had taken to picking me up from training. One day, though I'd asked her not to, she came in and watched the end of a training session. I dived well that day, not that she would have been able to tell. When the session was over, she approached Aleks, introduced herself, and asked him, 'So what do you think of my Joanie?'

To my surprise he was cordial with her. He told her I was an excellent diver. He told her I had a rare kind of potential. 'She's special.'

'I know,' Lou said, smiling at me like I was five.

'No, I mean – she has a rare talent, truly. I've coached plenty of girls, and she's something very special.'

'Seriously?' Lou didn't just say this with surprise but with disbelief. She looked at me and then back at Aleks. The nostalgic look on her face was gone. 'Are you sure?'

'Very seriously,' he said, speaking like I wasn't there. 'She's utterly fearless. You can't teach courage. Besides, I've never had anyone bury a dive like she can. I think she could go very far indeed.'

Lou took a moment, sizing him up, then looking at me, hard, as though searching for something she'd missed. Finally, she said, 'What do you mean, "bury"?'

He explained.

When you're diving, you aim for a rip entry. That's the kind of entry that makes no splash at all. When done correctly it's so quiet it's almost spooky – like a portal has opened up, like someone is moving seamlessly from one dimension to the next. It's all in the angle of the hands. They have to be flat, one on top of the other, the thumbs interlocked. They create a pocket of air that your body slips through.

It's called a rip entry because when you hit the water the sound is like a piece of paper being torn. Afterwards, the surface of the water looks like it's boiling. The thing is, the splash – the displaced water – is still there. But if you enter the water just right, you suck all the movement and mess under the water with you, rather than allowing anyone to see it.

I showered and met Lou at the car. It was her pride and joy: a black Mercedes coupé whose doors were grubby with makeup from all the times she had hastily rubbed foundation on her face before sprinting into a meeting or a deposition. I'd always been happy to be driven around in such luxury, but now, watching the other girls depart in their second-hand Hyundais and Mazdas, I felt a gnawing embarrassment. I didn't even have my learner's permit.

There was a jittering, buoyant energy about Lou. I didn't like it.

'What a smug fuck,' she said.

I shrugged. 'He's a good coach.'

'He got my hackles up. I don't trust him.'

'You don't have to trust him.'

'And who was that woman?'

'That's his wife.'

'You're shitting me.'

'Nope.'

'What's the story there?'

'Like I'd know.'

She started up the engine.

'Anyway,' Lou said, 'you might have warned me.'

'What do you mean?'

'Oh come on,' she said. She cupped her hand over her nose and mouth, attempted to smell her own breath. 'I wouldn't trust him, but – I would have brushed my teeth for that. Hell, I would have worn Spanx for that.'

'Gross.'

She looked into the side mirror, tried to make eye contact with my reflection.

'Don't tell me you don't see it.'

I wanted to change the subject. 'What are hackles, anyway?'

Lou didn't know either. She googled it while she drove.

'Erectile hairs along an animal's back, which rise when it is angry or alarmed,' she said. She ran her finger along the knobs of vertebrae at the back of her neck. 'Yep,' she said, satisfied. 'There they are.'

During a training session soon afterwards, Aleks told Camilla to take a new dive up to the platform. She'd been practising it on dry land for a while – the club had a foam pit and harnesses for this purpose. It was a 405B. A two-and-a-half inward somersault, in the pike position. Not a terrifying dive, by any means. But Camilla said, 'I can't.'

'Take it up,' Aleks said. His T-shirt was blue that day, but as clean and fresh as ever.

'But I'm not ready.'

'Take it up.'

'But —'

'Take it up, take it up, take it up, take it up …' Aleks kept saying it, over and over, until Camilla, clutching her chamois, made the climb to the platform.

I could tell right away that the dive was bad. Camilla baulked the takeoff, and kept her pretty green eyes closed all the way down. She hadn't even half come out of the dive when she hit the water. All of us winced. The splash was huge.

Julie, of course, filmed all of this. And when the team rushed to the pool's edge to check whether Camilla was okay, she filmed that too.

Camilla wasn't hurt; she was fine. But she got out of the pool crying and snivelling and went straight to the change-rooms. She was still in there when training finished, locked in a shower cubicle with the water running. It was Grace who comforted her, sitting outside the cubicle, talking to the gap beneath the shower door while slathering sorbolene on her legs.

'It's so unfair,' said Grace. 'He has no right to pressure you like that.'

But her fingers were busy on her own skin; she was admiring its slip, its sheen.

At the end of the next session, I was the first member of the squad to arrive in the room where we watched ourselves on video. Julie was there, setting up. She'd put straight blonde highlights in her straight brown hair. They weren't subtle. They were thin, painted-on stripes.

Camilla had quit the team. Aleks told us this, briefly, at the beginning of training. No-one had said anything, asked any questions. We proceeded as though she'd never been part of the team at all.

'Hi Joan,' said Julie. She was facing the black screen of the television. Her reflection looked even more gaunt and oblong than she did. The crystals on her jacket gleamed.

I wanted to know about Camilla; and more than this, I wanted to get a sense of the extent to which Julie Korsak bore her ill will. So I said, 'I feel so bad for Camilla,' and watched her reflected face for what it might betray.

She glanced at me and glanced away.

'To be honest,' she said, 'I thought she would have quit a long time ago.'

An image of the pool and the tower appeared on the screen. Julie Korsak turned and smiled at me, a warm maternal smile. Her tone became conspiratorial.

'Diving isn't for everyone, Joanie. You know that. You need courage.'

She fast-forwarded the video. Together we watched as I appeared in time-lapse onscreen, climbing the tower, then sprinting to its edge to throw myself into a forward dive.

'See?' Julie said. 'You have it. Courage.'

In the video, I surfaced from the deep water and dragged my weight out of the pool. Courage wasn't the word for what I had. But Julie Korsak didn't need to know that.

I might not have felt much sympathy for Camilla, but she was right to be scared. Diving can be fatal. When people think about the danger of diving, they think about Greg Louganis hitting his head on the board. But no-one really mentions Sergei Chalibashvili.

He was attempting the same dive for which Louganis is famous: the 307C. A reverse three-and-a-half somersault in the tuck position. 'Reverse' means that the diver is facing forward, but their somersault spins backwards, towards the platform. The margin for error is narrow; divers often look as though they're going to hit their heads, even when they don't.

Soon after the 307C was added to the competition table, it was attempted by both Louganis and Chalibashvili. Sergei jumped, didn't give himself enough room, and smacked the back of his skull on the concrete platform.

He was in a coma for a week, but never regained consciousness.

His coach was his mother. She never said a thing about it; she wasn't even there.

Lou didn't pay Aleks any serious attention until my first interstate tournament. She was between trials, so she decided to attend. And when she heard that our assistant coach wouldn't be there – Julie was having some kind of surgery, the nature of which not even Grace had been able to ferret out – she volunteered to come along and 'help'.

Lou told me this one morning after she'd come in without knocking to wake me up. She pulled the curtains open with one hand and threw a plate of toast onto my bed with the other. The toast slid onto the duvet. I picked up a slice and started eating it.

'I'll be your chaperone,' she said, amused.

'We're adults,' I told her. 'We don't need a chaperone.'

She laughed. She'd just washed her hair, and the wet strands of it were leaving dark patches on her blouse.

'Adults?' she said. 'You're not adults. You're *babies*.'

'You'll distract me.'

'I won't! You won't even know I'm there.'

'Why do you want to go, anyway? What are you going to do?'

She shrugged. 'Carry your bags. Cut up oranges. Console the losers.'

'Jesus Christ. We're not eight-year-olds.'

'Well, okay, maybe I'll take the videos,' she said. She mussed my hair with her buttery hands. 'Isn't that what horse-face Julie does?'

Lou even left her Mercedes behind, opting to travel with us in the minibus Aleks had hired. She sat across the aisle from him, at the front, behind the driver. I sat close to the back. Grace sat behind me.

I had planned to put my headphones on, close my eyes, and speak to no-one. Instead I found myself with my eyes half open, like a lizard, watching Aleks talk to my sister.

'She's pretty,' said a voice behind me.

I turned. 'What?'

'Your mum.'

Grace leaned forward so I could see her face in the gap between the seats.

'She's not my mum. She's my sister.'

Grace knew this. 'Oh yeah,' she said. 'That's right. Well, she's pretty, anyway.'

'I guess.'

'You don't think so?'

'I don't think about it.'

'He thinks she's pretty,' Grace said.

I said nothing. Grace waited a minute before she spoke again.

'I mean, it makes sense. Now Camilla's gone …'

'*What?*'

'I'm just saying – he has a type. That's all.'

'She doesn't even look like Camilla.'

'Sure,' said Grace. 'Whatever you say.'

We fell into silence then, a silence in which I replayed every interaction I'd ever seen between Aleks and Lou.

I remembered one evening when I was late getting out of training. I had drilled my set of five dives over and over, thirty times or more. My wrists were throbbing.

Lou had parked in a disabled space, and Aleks's modest sedan was in the space next to her. Lou had kept the engine running. Lou always kept the engine running.

She had the window rolled down despite the chill. She was eating from a bucket of KFC, using her teeth to tear the crusted skin. There was a pile of bones between her car and his. She must have been waiting a while.

I threw my bag in the footwell and got in the car.

'Want some chicken?'

She held out the piece she was eating. Half of it was gone. The darker flesh and strings of sinew were visible, the grey-purple bone exposed.

'No.'

'Suit yourself,' Lou said, taking another bite.

When she'd picked the leg clean, she licked her fingers and thumbs and made a little humph noise of satisfaction. She wiped her hands on the refresher towelette and used it to swipe the last of her lipstick off before throwing the bucket and towelette out the car window.

'Lou!'

'What?'

'Forget it.'

'Do I smell like chicken? Smell my hair.'

She bent her head. I leaned over and sniffed. She did smell like chicken, a rich, fatty, savoury smell. Beneath that, there were the usual Lou smells: cigarette smoke, dry cleaning, the powdery perfume she wore which gave me a headache.

'Well?'

'You're fine.'

There was movement in front of the car. Aleks was leaving for the night, his gym bag slung across his body.

He approached his car, saw the scattered chicken bones, then gave Lou a curt nod.

Lou nodded in return, holding eye contact.

'Keep walking, pretty boy,' she said under her breath.

I'd taken her tone as wary, circumspect. I thought she was being protective of me, that she sensed in Aleks the same tendencies she saw in her clients.

But maybe I'd been wrong. It was hard to know; Lou never seemed interested in men. She'd never had a boyfriend, at least not one I'd met. Sometimes she would go to a bar, find a man, go back to his place and roll out of there while it was still dark, never to speak to him again. She'd taken the morning-after pill so many times that she had chronic rashes and her period had become unpredictable. But that was the extent of her love life.

On the bus, she and Aleks kept talking. At one point Lou threw her head back and laughed. I closed my eyes and tried to picture myself on the ten-metre platform, everyone else far away and too small to matter.

Perhaps it was due to these distractions that I performed so disastrously. I ranked outside of the top twelve in my event, getting nowhere near the finals. In the hotel room that night I sat on the shower floor with the water running for half an hour, imagining how it would feel to punch through the shower screen. Then I wrapped myself in the scratchy hotel robe and joined Grace, who was flicking between channels.

She was drinking a Gatorade.

'Good shower?'

My reply was a grunt. I could smell the Gatorade – an off smell somewhere between grape juice and seawater. Grace had somehow made it out of that competition with a bronze medal, which she now wore over her own hotel robe. This only added to my indignation. Grace was a decent diver; I was better.

'Do you think he's mad at me?' I asked.

'Who, ballsack?'

This was her name for Aleks.

'Yeah. Him.'

Grace burped.

'Probably,' she said, her eyes fixed on the TV. 'You bombed.'

On the closing night of the competition, there was a dinner for the athletes and their families. Lou was running late, as always. She arrived in a flurry, wearing a dress made of a dark, stretchy, spangled material which showed how thin she was. It had a dip in the back where you could see the sharpness of her shoulder blades, the sun damage she'd collected.

She sat with the parents. I was on a table with my teammates. Usually we'd be sipping mineral water and refusing the bread and butter, but I was sulking and ate everything in sight.

Dinner was an alternate drop. For dessert I was given chocolate cake. Next to me, Grace had lemon meringue pie. I ate my cake unselfconsciously. It was as sweet and stodgy as I'd hoped it would be. It stuck to the roof of my mouth and I sucked it down. I wrapped my tongue around my spoon to collect the last flecks of cream.

'Good?' Grace asked.

She'd pushed her pie away. I didn't know how long she'd been watching.

'It's okay.'

'Looked like you were enjoying it.'

She nudged the pie over to me. 'Here,' she said. 'I'm not going to eat it.'

I'd been casting a few looks towards Lou during the evening: there she was, checking her phone. Picking her teeth. Downing a glass of champagne in a single gulp. Loosening the knot of dark hair on top of her head, then tying it up again. I couldn't tell if she was ignoring the parents at the table or they were ignoring her; either way, she didn't seem to be talking to them.

A band was playing, a group of forty-somethings in cheap suits doing sexless covers of the Rolling Stones and Marvin Gaye. Hardly any of the athletes were dancing. Those who were looked strange, the muscles they'd cultivated suddenly asked to be flippant. Their bodies were overqualified for this. It was embarrassing. I watched the half-hearted shuffling and grinding while I drank a cup of bitter filtered coffee.

Then, to my horror, there was Lou, and she was dancing with Aleks. She was tipsy; I could see that in the high colour in her cheeks, and the way her face had relaxed out of its habitual grimace into a smile that was someone else's: someone young and carefree. Aleks held one of her hands. His other hand was on her hip.

The song ended. There was a smattering of applause, and then Lou wandered to the bathroom, the same stupid smile on her face.

I followed her.

'Hey, there you are,' she said when she saw me. She pulled me into her chest and kissed the top of my head. I could smell the champagne and the perfume, the sweat, the faint chargrilled remains of the steak she'd eaten.

'He has a wife. Remember?' I said.

Lou pulled back. 'Who has a wife?'

'I'm serious.'

She walked to the sink, turned the tap on full and splashed water on her face. She grabbed a handful of paper towels and wiped away the makeup that had gathered under her eyes. Suddenly, she seemed sober.

'They're separating, actually. Not that it's any of your business,' she said.

'Since when?'

'It's recent.' She pointed to her own left hand. 'See for yourself. No ring.'

'You don't even like him,' I said. 'You said he couldn't be trusted. Remember?'

She walked to the bin and pitched the paper towels in.

'What's the matter, Joanie? Jealous?'

She seemed drunk again, swaying a little in her stilettos. She gave me a crooked, triumphant smile and left the bathroom.

I washed my hands, though they weren't dirty. I looked at my face in the mirror, under the fluorescent lights, and then, in order to look somewhere else, I read the nearby sign about the importance of thorough handwashing. It warned about germs, about how careful you have to be to avoid them. It gave a number of helpful tips: rub your hands together for twenty seconds. Use plenty of soap. Clean beneath your fingernails. And always wash beneath your rings. Underneath a ring, it said, there are more germs than there are people in Europe.

I went back to the table and ate Grace's lemon meringue pie. I scraped up the ice cream, which had melted all over the plate.

'Naughty girl,' said Grace. Her face looked as dry as ever.

As I left, they were still dancing. But if something happened that night, Lou never mentioned it. And I didn't ask.

At the end of the first training session after the competition, Aleks asked me to come to his office. My heart was skidding when I went in, though I wasn't sure where I should focus my apprehension – would he want to discuss my diving or my sister?

'Joan,' he said. 'Have a seat.'

His office was usually tidy but now it was a mess: papers all over the desk, folders, his whistle on its fraying black nylon rope. In one corner of the room there was a bouquet of red and yellow pool noodles tied with a string. I realised that it must have been Julie who kept the place clean for him. I glanced at his hand: no ring.

I considered the possibility that he would do what Grace said he'd done with Camilla: lock the door, twist the venetian blinds closed. But no. He shut the door, then returned to his seat. I had a whiff of his marine-smelling aftershave as he passed me.

'Last weekend,' he said. I watched his Adam's apple bounce in his throat. It gave me the urge to swallow. 'What happened?'

'I don't know,' I said. What I understood about my terrible performance was more an impression than an explanation. Unnerved by him and by Lou, by their proximity to one another, I'd felt half in and half out of my own body, and had the sense that I would have been able to dive competently if I'd occupied one or the other space fully. Instead it felt like I was fighting to put myself on or take myself off. Of course, there was no way of communicating this to Aleks, so I said again, 'I don't know.'

Then I started crying. There was no build-up, no trembling lower lip. The tears came out immediately, like a sneeze. I was horrified.

He plucked a tissue from a box and held it out to me; when I didn't take it, staunching my nose with my fingers, he let the tissue go and it floated elegantly into my lap.

'Enough,' he said.

I dared a look at him but I couldn't read his expression. Behind Aleks's head there was a portrait of him as a younger man, executing a dive in competition – there was no platform in the photo and no water, just the tan twist of his body against a pale blue sky.

'Now you know how it feels. Real competition. Now you know what it's like when someone rattles your cage. They're all doing it, you know. The other teams. Even your own team.'

I thought of Grace and her medal, her Gatorade, how she'd jerked her ankle, flapping the hotel slipper against the sole of her foot over and over again.

'I don't mind you failing,' Aleks continued. 'This time. I think it will be like a splinter in your finger. I think a little humiliation will do you the world of good.'

When I got home and told Lou about the meeting, she said, 'He meant humility.'

I thought about how, when he'd finished speaking, he'd risen and come over to my side of the desk. He tapped my head and then my shoulder, pat pat, pat pat, like I was a friend's dog he felt obligated to pet.

'No,' I said, 'he didn't.'

Perhaps the humiliation was good for me. Driven by spite, I came to training sessions with a newer, deeper sense of focus. I did additional weights sessions, alone in the gym that was attached to the aquatic centre. I actually followed the plan for recovery and stretching I had been given, instead of ignoring it. As the weeks passed, I improved. And when we watched the videos of our dives, I was so critical of my own performance – 'My pelvis is rotated'; 'I need to relax my shoulders'; 'My toes are curling back' – that often Aleks was left with nothing to say.

In our next competition I won a silver medal.

'Congratulations,' said Grace.

'Thanks,' I said. 'Better luck next time.'

She shook her head and smiled grimly.

'Fuck you, Joan,' she said.

Before doing what I had made my mind up to do, I waited until Lou was in the middle of another trial. And this one promised to be particularly complex. A man – only barely a man, he was my age – had sent text messages containing pornographic photos to his girlfriend, who was three years younger. The parents had gotten the police involved.

'How bad was the porn?' I'd asked. This was always a crucial question.

'Bad. Tentacles.'

She'd slipped her fingers beneath her glasses and rubbed the skin around her eyes.

I told Lou I could take the bus home until the trial was over.

I also waited for a day when Julie wasn't there. Such days were becoming more frequent. Grace suspected that her surgery was in fact a facelift, which hadn't gone well, and that her absences were related to attempts to have the damage reversed. She kept saying, 'Look at her ears, Joan! It's so fucking obvious!' I looked for the signs Grace saw – scars, bald patches – but couldn't see anything.

On the day I chose, I waited in the carpark, having smeared cherry balm on my lips and dried my hair beneath the hand dryer in the change-rooms. Finally, Aleks appeared.

'Joan?' he said. His keys were jingling in his hand. 'You okay?'

The breeze made my skin turn to gooseflesh. I'd sprayed some of Lou's perfume on my neck and down my underpants, and the bottle was wrapped in a wet towel at the top of my bag.

I walked over to where he stood, near his car, and he smiled.

'You need a ride somewhere?'

I hadn't planned on this development, but it suited me.

'Yeah. Lou's at work.'

This mention of my sister hung in the air between us for a moment.

'Come on,' Aleks said. 'I'll take you home.'

I put my bag in the back, then settled into the passenger seat of his dull, functional sedan. It shifted when he sat his own weight in the driver's seat. He slipped his key in the ignition, but hesitated before turning it.

'That perfume …' he said, turning to me.

I didn't answer. All it took was that tiny lean from Aleks and I swooped in.

In my daydreams I'd decided how I would like things to proceed, down to a level of granular detail I'd never applied to my studies, or, until recently, to my diving. When my lips touched his he would pull back for a moment, his eyes scanning the surrounding area.

'Everyone's gone,' I'd say.

He'd put his hands around my wrists, say, 'Stop. We can't do this.'

He'd have to show a little hesitation. What kind of man would he be otherwise?

'I could lose my job,' he'd say.

But then his eyes would move to my lips, and he'd kiss me, and I would be shocked at the sheer force of it. I'd kissed boys before, but boys were sloppy, and needy, like dogs. Aleks would kiss me and I would understand that it was a skill, that there were techniques to be learned and applied. So this is how it's done, I'd think, and I'd catch on to kissing as quickly as I caught on to turning a somersault.

'We're supposed to discourage you, you know,' he'd say, breathless. 'From boys.'

'I know,' I'd reply, slipping my hand under his shirt. 'They're a distraction.'

Unfortunately, things did not proceed as I'd imagined. It would be better for him, I suppose, if I could say his rejection was swift and definitive. But there was a returned pressure, almost an involuntary response, from his lips. His hand covered one breast and gave a quick, experimental squeeze, as if he were testing a peach or an avocado. Then he pulled away, thoughtfully, without haste, and seemed to reconsider.

He turned the key in the ignition.

'Maybe you should get the bus,' he said, staring straight ahead.

I said nothing. I got out of the car and went to retrieve my gym bag, feeling a sudden and intense heat in my cheeks. I didn't hurry. If he could take his time, so could I.

I thought about what had happened all the way home on the bus. I'd only managed to touch him briefly, but I comforted myself by thinking that his body was even less suited for diving than I'd realised. I'd run my fingers up his spine; it curved to the left.

A few days later, Lou came home and told me the tentacle trial was over. She cracked open a bottle of Midori and kicked off her shoes and was soon on the couch drinking, her tongue a bright witch-green.

'What happened?'

'Six months suspended. Five years probation. He'll be on the sex offenders register.'

'Too bad you didn't win.'

She furrowed her brow. 'Joanie, that is a win.'

Then we heard our gate swing shut. We looked at each other. No-one ever came to our house.

'Go and hide,' Lou said.

This is the deal we have. If a stranger approaches the house I have to hide. It's one of the consequences of Lou's dealings with perverts. Occasionally her clients have appeared at the front door, but Lou is much more worried about the family members of victims. They've graffitied the house before, left threatening notes about how they'll kill her and what they'll do to her body.

I went to Lou's room at the front of the house and peeked out from behind the curtains.

It was Julie Korsak. She had a smile plastered onto her face. She was carrying a plastic bag, clutching it with both hands.

Had she had a facelift? I couldn't tell.

The bell rang. Lou padded down the hallway and opened the door. I stayed where I was.

'Mrs Korsak?'

'That's right. And you're Joan's mother, aren't you?'

'More or less.'

'In any case – I wanted to return something of yours,' she said.

Lou reached for the bag but Julie, though she kept smiling, held onto it.

'This was in my car,' she said, showing Lou what the bag contained.

'In your car?'

Julie nodded, and kept nodding like she couldn't stop.

Lou snatched the bag. She closed the door in Julie's face, then turned and walked straight down to the kitchen. I followed.

'What was that about?' I said. 'What happened? Lou? Lou?'

She rounded on me, furious. She threw the bag at me.

It contained her perfume.

'Idiot,' she snarled, and I had a glimpse of what she must be like in court, eviscerating accusers as they sat quivering in the dock. 'Don't you see what you've done? You absolute little *idiot.*'

She picked up a glass and threw it into the shallow, dirty water in the sink. She threw it so hard it smashed.

For a while after that Lou and I weren't speaking. And Aleks, at training, only spoke to me to issue a command or a correction.

'What's up his ass?' Grace said, with her usual radar for drama.

I shrugged.

I was working on a new dive. A 5253B. A back two-and-a-half somersault with one-and-a-half twists, in the pike position. A difficult dive, but one I'd have to know if I ever wanted to join an elite squad. I'd been preparing it for a while, but hadn't yet taken it up to the platform. In fact, I was beginning to suspect Aleks was holding me back on purpose; some kind of revenge for the trouble I'd caused.

One day, I told him I was ready. 'I've been ready for weeks,' I said.

'I'll tell you when you're ready,' he said.

I continued the training session, drilling my competition dives over and over. But as I jumped and flipped and twisted, I could feel my anger seething. Aleks gave corrections, but otherwise didn't acknowledge me. I thought of his hand on my breast, of my gnawing, unanswered question: what had made him refuse me?

As for what happened next, I've seen Julie's footage. There I am, back to the water, ready to attempt the 5253B. My body is tense – I can see how taut my abdomen is, how deeply I'm breathing into that concave space, which inflates and deflates in time with my breath. And then my arms swing out and I push off from the platform. The takeoff is all wrong. Not high enough. Not far enough away from the platform.

I didn't come out in time. I was never going to. I didn't know where the pool was. I've freeze-framed the whole dive, trying to isolate the moment that my nose smashes against the surface of the water. Water is so pliable, they warn us, until you hit it at full speed. Then it might as well be concrete.

I'm under a few seconds before someone dives in after me. I've seen it a hundred times: I am a dark ball of shadow, and then there's a shocking bright cloud as blood starts rushing from my nose.

As for the injuries, they weren't catastrophic – other than a broken nose, there was just a lot of bruising, on my face and on my flank. Bruises so deep they took days to reach the surface.

When I got out of the pool, blood was pouring down my body, down my chest and legs, the red thinning to yellow as it was diluted by the water.

I sat down on a white plastic chair and let it run onto the floor.

Aleks came over. He stood close. He reached out and pinched my nose shut, and I felt my nostrils fill with blood.

'Does that hurt?' he said.

'No,' I said, looking up at him. 'I can't feel a thing.'

Lou never told me how she convinced Julie Korsak to send her the file. That file would have exonerated her husband; in it, you can see me asking to attempt the dive, and you can see Aleks's refusal.

I don't know if Lou made promises, or threats; I don't know if she found a weak spot, a tender spot on Julie Korsak's person, and pushed it. All I know is that we ended up with it and Aleks didn't.

I found it strange to watch that video, given the circumstances. It was weird to see myself through Julie Korsak's eyes. It gave me a chance to feel the way she must have felt about my sister, about me. Hers was a different kind of anger than mine or Lou's. It was pure, in a way. It was the anger of someone who knows she's in the right.

I didn't see the letter Lou wrote until many years later. But it was as excoriating as she could be. *I have grave concerns about the suitability of this man*, she wrote. She said she had reason to believe he'd behaved inappropriately. And now I'd received a serious injury under his care. She said he'd pushed me, pressured me, that he might have done untold psychological damage. She had reason to believe I wasn't the first girl he'd hurt.

Was the club just going to let this stand? Let this man take young women interstate, possibly even overseas? Young women whose minds hadn't formed, who were trusting and impressionable?

I suppose they never looked up Lou's record regarding girls and the men who took advantage of them, because a disciplinary meeting was immediately called. Lou was invited. I wasn't. Grace texted me: *shit's about to hit the fan*.

I didn't answer.

I waited in the Mercedes while Lou went into the meeting. I sat there with my bandaged nose and watched her striding towards the glass doors. I almost felt sorry for Aleks. He would end up like the piece of cheese that woman in the deli had fed through the machine, pulverised into dust.

Now that I think of it, it isn't quite right to say that Lou and I hadn't been speaking since Julie Korsak's visit to our house. That night, and several other nights that followed, I climbed into Lou's bed with its filthy, expensive sheets.

She was curled up on her side. She didn't even open her eyes. She reached out blindly behind her, touching my face, patting my hair.

'Nightmare?' she said.

'Nightmare,' I said.

While I was recovering, I often thought of Sergei Chalibashvili. But I thought about Greg Louganis too. Half an hour after Chalibashvili's accident, Louganis jumped into that pool, still tinged brown from Chalibashvili's blood.

He said he'd had a premonition when his rival climbed to the platform. He'd just known something would go wrong.

Louganis completed the 307C anyway. He went on to win an Olympic medal with that dive.

Lou drove me to my first training session back. She kept humming and put her foot down hard on the accelerator. The car purred and shot ahead.

'I love this car,' she said.

I remembered the day she'd bought it. She picked me up from school with the windows down and music blaring. I looked at the low, black, sleek coupé and said, 'What if you need to fit more than two people?'

Lou looked at me like I was crazy.

'Who else would I need to fit?' she said.

My first dive from the ten-metre platform was a simple forward dive, pike position, no somersaults, no twists. I felt weaker, sluggish. I didn't get nearly enough lift. The angle was all wrong. It would take time to get back to the way I had been. And with Aleks gone, I doubted I'd be able to maintain my previous level of motivation.

Still, I put my hands the right way. Flat palms, straight arms pressing into my ears, one hand over the other. I kept my eyes open. Here was the water; I smashed through and vanished under it. There was the familiar cold, the familiar sting of impact.

As I was sinking, the thought occurred to me: the water didn't care. It didn't care if I was facing up to something. If I was making up for something. It didn't care about the mistakes I'd made or the crimes I'd committed. The water would do what it had always done: break my fall, and drag me back to the surface.

Exchange

Whenever anyone asked, she said that Billy had gone on an exchange. He had gone to Switzerland, she said. He was staying with a lovely host family, Hans and Helga Fischer, and their daughter, Marcia, who was Billy's age. The Fischers lived in Zurich. They went skiing on weekends. They had a large hound named Bruno who was fond of her son. There was every chance that Billy and Marcia would share a tender and appropriate first love.

She found a postcard of Zurich, its buildings iced with fresh snow, and stuck it on her fridge.

As the weeks went by, she found herself thinking of Zurich while she was on the bus to see Billy. She'd picture the Fischer family rolling with their dog in the snow, carolling with their neighbours at Christmas, drinking mulled wine in front of a log fire.

She'd think of them as she opened the fridge to find a single egg to boil for her dinner, and when she shrank and huddled her body under the cold sheets, trying to warm the bed.

After a time she began to envy her son, to envy the memories, so clear in her mind, of his exchange. She'd flick through them like a series of snapshots – Billy outside a historic church; Billy on skis, waving, his hands in thick red mittens; Billy grinning, young and pink-cheeked, Marcia's smiling face pressed into his shoulder.

Joyriders

Maybe it stuck in my mind because I heard there were two boys and a girl and my work crew was the same: two boys, me and Curtis, and one girl. Erica.

Erica was drinking a 7-Eleven cappuccino when we first heard about the joyriders. We were at the depot waiting for the day's work order. I watched her pour three packets of white sugar into her coffee, one after the other, and stir it with a plastic straw.

'That stuff will kill you,' I said.

She didn't even look up.

Two boys, one girl, all under eighteen. That's what they told us. They had tied scarves around their faces and worn baseball caps and sunglasses and robbed three service stations using weapons that looked like they could have been found in someone's kitchen, someone's garage: a knife, a box cutter, a screwdriver with a pink handle. One of them always sat at the wheel of their stolen, plate-less car, revving the engine, waiting to scream off down the highway.

On the way out of one petrol station, they had sideswiped another car and sent it rolling onto the verge. They hadn't stopped to see what damage they'd done.

My crew's job was to clean up their mess.

We live on an island that most people try to leave. It is bisected by a single, nearly straight highway, which connects two towns that call themselves cities. You can go a while without passing anyone on that highway. When it's dark, people drive with their high beams on. They only turn them down at the last second, when they're about to pass you. Sometimes they don't turn them down at all and the night goes blind-white for a moment as they flash past.

We left the depot and drove a couple of hours up the highway to where the crash had taken place. The mood in the truck was cheerful. Not because the driver in the other car hadn't died, although he hadn't; the airbags had deployed, and soon enough we'd all be sneezing out the fine powder that spent airbags leave over everything.

No – we were excited because petrol stations are where people tend to lose stuff. Things left on top of a car, things that slide off the dash and out an open window. Wallets, phones, cash, sunglasses. We'd found a prosthetic leg once, wearing a white sneaker that looked brand-new.

The agreement we have – me, Erica, Curtis – is that whatever we find we split evenly. Pirate's rules, that's what Erica calls it. One man, one share. It means that when someone accidentally rides the mower over a loose twenty-dollar note and the fragments shoot out in a bright orange burst, we all lose $6.70 or thereabouts.

Sometimes we talk about how we might strike it rich one day; find a suitcase full of cash, or diamonds, or bars of gold bullion.

'You never know,' I say. 'It could happen.'

'How good would that be,' says Curtis.

I snap my fingers. 'I'd be out of here like *that*.'

'Don't get your hopes up,' says Erica.

By the time we reached the scene of the accident, the cops were gone, the ambulances were gone, the driver was gone.

We surveyed the scene: tyre marks bending and stuttering across the white lines of the road, bluish glass that turned to crumbs rather than shattering. A hubcap, a mirror.

It wasn't the worst I'd seen, not by a long shot. Even so, I had to hose the blood off the road and into the weeds that lined the highway.

'You're fertilising them, you know,' Erica said. She nodded towards the foaming blood-water mixture and the tangled spread of gorse and boneseed and Spanish heath that was already soaking it up.

I wasn't sure if she was joking. But it made me imagine all those weeds by the side of the road shooting up and thickening and flowering. It made me think of something we'd been taught: a weed is any plant that grows where it isn't wanted.

'Find anything?' Curtis asked when we were back in the truck.

'Nah. You?'

He and Erica hadn't found much either, he told me: a few coins, gold as well as silver; a packet of cigarettes with two stale ones left rolling around inside.

Keeping the grass on the verge short is one of our regular jobs. So is weeding. So is scooping up the flung and flattened bodies of kangaroos and wombats, and the myna birds and magpies and crows whose wings still catch the wind though their bodies have been pasted into the bitumen.

We're supposed to check the pouches of the native animals we find. It's always Curtis who does this, putting on a pair of gloves and stretching out the pouches while Erica and I stand by making dirty jokes. Sometimes he finds something still alive. We call the wildlife service, which sends a carer to pick them up.

Curtis doesn't have to sit with those animals, but he does. He wraps them in the towels he keeps in the truck.

'Most of them won't make it,' Erica says.

'I know,' Curtis replies, but he does it anyway.

That day, after cleaning up the accident, we were sent further north. There are crops of opium poppies up there. They look pretty in the springtime, the poppies – the flowers bloom so white and so thick they look like frost.

We'd been sent to mow the grass along a section of road that had poppy fields rolling out on either side. There's less security than you'd think around those fields: just some wire boundary fences, and signs that say *Danger! Lethal!* The crops are supposed to be patrolled, but I've never seen any guards.

Curtis claims to have eaten the resin that comes from the poppies. He says he went in once and got away with a whole bunch of seed pods rolled in his shirt.

It would be easy enough to do. Sometimes we're so close you could reach an arm through the fence and touch the flowers.

Curtis says what you do is make cuts in the pod and wait for the latex to ooze out. And when it does, you keep waiting until it turns thick and brown-black, and then you roll a little bit into a ball between your fingertips and eat it.

'What's it like?' I asked.

'It's like being dead,' he said. 'In a good way.'

Curtis told me that when he'd finally come down he realised he'd been lying still on his unmade bed for sixteen hours. He'd heard his housemates calling, but hadn't been able to answer. He'd been too far away, drifting outside his own mind, his own body. He said he'd never been happier.

But that day he ignored the poppies. We all did. That day, like most of our days, was spent mowing, and picking up rubbish: crushed cans, chip packets, used condoms, wads of gum. Sometimes people screamed things at us from moving cars. This was typical. Usually they were going too fast to be understood. Sometimes, though, you'd hear a word: fucken, loser, shit. Or, if they'd seen Erica: bitch, fat, cunt.

Sometimes they threw things: beer bottles, burgers that released a pale green spray of shredded lettuce. Once, a guy threw a carton of strawberry milk at Erica. It hit her square in the back. She barely reacted. She speared the container and put it into a garbage bag. The milk had soaked into the lengths of her hair. By the end of the day her hair had dried and frizzed and there was a stink rolling off her: sweet fake strawberry mixed with the sour-udder smell of the milk.

But none of us complained. We just rolled the windows down and drove home in silence.

I told Curtis I didn't find anything at the crash site, but that's because I found something I didn't want to share. It was while

I was hosing that I saw it. A wallet. Yellow, almost as yellow as the gorse, with grime worked into the texture of the leather. I checked – the others weren't watching. I picked it up and slipped it into the waistband of my pants.

I didn't mention it to anyone, and when I returned that night to the chilly linoleum of my flat I pulled everything out of the wallet and examined it.

It was all intact: credit cards, black and red and platinum. Health insurance. Gym membership. Driver's licence. Frequent flyer memberships for the three airlines that flew people off this island. Perfume sample cards, their scent faded.

And in the folds at the back: $865.

The licence belonged to a woman born in the same year as me. She looked both younger and older than I did. Older because her hair was neat and smooth and she wore diamonds in her ears. But younger, because even in that hazy photo you could tell she had soft, indoor skin; her face didn't have the windburned, thickened look that it gets when you work outside.

I went to bed, and when I slipped my hand into my boxer shorts my palm had the smell of her wallet on it: leather, perfume, crisp notes fresh from the ATM.

The next day was my day off. I drove to her house, which was in a nice suburb. I'd made an effort. I wore my good jeans, a clean T-shirt. I rang the bell.

When she opened the door she kept the security screen locked.

'Can I help you?'

'Hi,' I said. I knew instantly – from the way she backed up, the look on her face – that I'd made a mistake. 'I think I found your wallet.'

I held it out to the mesh of the screen door. She waited for a moment before opening it.

'Thank you.'

'You can check,' I said. 'Everything's there.'

I didn't think she'd do it. But I stood and watched as she examined all her cards and counted the notes.

'Thank you,' the woman said again. She cleared her throat. 'I hope you haven't gone too far out of your way.'

'No,' I said. 'It's nothing.'

I turned to go, but she said, 'Hang on a second.'

She padded down the polished floorboards in her hallway, and came back holding a six-pack of beer that had two bottles missing. She handed it to me.

'For your trouble,' she said.

Maybe I should have had some pride and waved them away, but before I knew it the icy brown glass was pressing into my abdomen and I was holding them the way Curtis held those baby animals.

I opened one as soon as I got home. It wasn't the type of beer that got thrown at us from car windows. It was good beer. It tasted of something more than the sour tang of alcohol. I drank the bottles one after another until all of them were gone.

Sometimes I think it's inevitable that I will end up with Erica. If that happened I don't know which of us would be more disappointed.

Maybe it's better to be like Curtis, to believe that one day we'll find a duffel bag full of cash and all our problems will vanish, the way a car vanishes when it turns its headlights off.

Perhaps that's what they did, those kids who'd kept tearing up and down the highway that runs like an old scar down the centre of this island. Perhaps they turned the headlights off and that's why things ended how they ended.

At least, I assumed it was them. It was the morning after I'd returned the wallet and still so dark and cold it may as well have been the middle of the night. We'd received our work order. A car had hit a truck, thrown two of its passengers, wrapped itself around a tree.

Had anyone survived? No-one knew.

On the way to the accident site, we stopped to clear a wallaby from the middle of the road. I turned the headlights down and kept the truck running while Curtis got out and knelt on the asphalt. He felt around inside the pouch. We didn't make any jokes.

He dragged the wallaby to the side of the road. We do that to protect the scavengers – eagles, quolls, devils – that come to eat the dead and become roadkill in turn.

He walked back to the truck wiping one gloved hand on his trousers.

'Anything?' Erica said after he got into the back seat and slammed the door.

He shook his head. If there had been something in there, it wasn't something he could save.

I put the truck into gear and switched on the high beams. All the invisible trees were suddenly there, white and panicked, waving their arms. We ignored them. I put my foot down and kept on driving.

The One You've Been Waiting For

Our neighbours thought we didn't know we'd bought the murder house. But we knew. The discount we'd received on the place was in proportion to the horror that had happened there. Meaning: it was so cheap even we could afford it. And suddenly, as Tate put it, we were 'in'.

'In what?'

'In a good area. With good people.'

'What does that mean? "Good people"?'

'Don't be obtuse.'

'I'm not.'

But Tate was right; I was being obtuse. I too felt thrilled to be living in the kind of area where someone might have a wine cellar or a panic room. But the thrill was accompanied by a certain trepidation. I felt I should approach the house with humility; with my head bowed and a preparedness to genuflect. That way, if it contained any restless spirits, they would be assuaged. Or at least, they'd direct their rage towards Tate instead of me.

Tate sensed that I was treating the house with a certain reverence. But he mistook it for a fear of the house, of what had happened there.

'It doesn't bother you, does it?' he'd asked before we put in an offer.

'The murder thing?'

'Yeah. The murder thing.'

'It should bother us. Don't you think?'

'It won't make us more likely to be murdered, if that's what you're worried about,' Tate said. 'If anything, we're less likely to be murdered in that house. How often would murders happen twice in the same house?'

My reckoning of the probabilities was different. But I didn't demur.

'Besides,' Tate said, 'you know what I think about being a victim.'

Tate had a genuine belief that it was impossible for anyone to murder him because of his mindset. He didn't have the attitude of a victim; therefore he wouldn't become one. Tate stopped short of articulating the corollary of this theory – that murder victims had somehow brought their misfortune on themselves – but it was implied nevertheless.

Murder, however, was not the cause of my concern. Something Tate didn't know was that I believed in ghosts, genuinely and wholeheartedly. It was the potential ghosts who both worried me and attracted me to the house.

I dated this fascination to the time when a girl from my school – not in my year, she was in year twelve while I was in year eight – suddenly died. Georgia. She hadn't been ill, hadn't suffered an accident. She just died one night in her sleep.

'That happens with young people sometimes,' I heard one of

the teachers, comfortably in her fifties and out of danger, say to another. 'They just go to sleep and don't wake up.'

At a number of slumber parties afterwards, other girls and I would try to summon Georgia's ghost. We held seances, lighting candles, joining hands, closing our eyes, chanting. One girl's liberal-minded parents even bought her a ouija board for her birthday, and we'd sit there with our fingers on the planchette, asking questions.

We asked Georgia if she was in the room, and the planchette always slid to yes.

We asked Georgia if she'd kissed a boy before she died and she said yes.

We asked Georgia if it hurt to die and she said no.

Everyone was giddy and nervous, but gradually, through a certain quality to their shrieks and shudders, I came to realise I was the only one there harbouring a genuine belief that Georgia's ghost was real, and truly wanted to speak with us. I always expected to see Georgia, perhaps translucent and in a fluttering nightgown, strands of her hair rising like she was channelling static. I would pray to her, cobbling together parts of other prayers: Dear Georgia, *proteggimi*, now and in the hour of my death.

We asked, once, which of us would die next.

I held my breath, certain she would spell out my name. Instead the planchette slid to B. Then E. She spelled out Bethany. I looked over at Bethany with a new and abiding disgust.

As an adult, I sometimes still thought of Georgia, still imagined I might call her up; I hoped to see her at the end of my bed, or behind me in the clearing steam in the bathroom mirror.

The house was at the bottom of a cul-de-sac that sloped downwards as if into a dell. There were trees growing on the nature strip: an English oak, a Monterey cypress, several eucalypts. All the houses on that street had names, even the ones that had been built in recent years: Arundel, Jettysprite, Currawong … The fences were like walls, high and smooth, made from stone or concrete slabs. When we'd attended the inspection, the fence outside the murder house had a billboard attached. Its headline read: THIS IS THE ONE YOU'VE BEEN WAITING FOR.

Everything was so private, so dignified. We could be dignified too, I thought, living in a place like this.

No ghosts appeared when we moved in. But neighbours did. When they first came over, they wandered through, saying polite things: 'So much natural light!' 'That garden will be gorgeous come spring!' And, most often of all: 'I just love what you've done with the place.'

We went through the little pantomime, seeming gormless and enthused about our good luck. We told them we thought it must have had vermin, generations of rats and the dust of their ancestors, termites patiently hollowing out the foundations. We thought it must have been full of rot, or a spreading lace of black mould we'd somehow missed during inspection. How else could we get so lucky? That's what Tate would say. Then he'd smile: at me, at them, at the cornices, the walls, the electric kettle with its transparent window through which you could see the water hit a rolling boil.

If you want to know what people do when they walk into a murder house, I'll tell you. They look around, pointing out things they're not interested in while their gazes sweep the room for traces of the evidence. Blood spatter, perhaps, brain matter, shards of bone, dents in the wall to indicate a struggle. But the place was spotless. New paint. New appliances. New floors. In some rooms, new windows. The real estate agent had been surprisingly frank about all of this. He'd said, 'I want you to know what you're getting into. I don't want there to be any nasty surprises.'

'Is that a Smeg?' Tate had asked, staring at the chrome oven. He looked at me with an expression of absolute sincerity. 'I've always wanted a Smeg.'

Tate worked in sales. He sold advertising for a suite of websites directed at 'liquid' men. This did not mean what I had initially pictured: men made from ice or quicksilver, melting or darting about on the floor. It meant men with ready disposable income. There were websites on fitness, grooming, how to talk to women. It was all run out of a small office on the tenth floor of a building in the city that looked out onto another floor of offices where similar men at similar desks stared back at Tate and his colleagues.

Tate spent his days on the phone with businesses that sold protein powders or bespoke suits, beard oils, spy cameras, home-brew kits, body sprays. Anyone, Tate said, who could offer life-enhancing products to the aspirational modern gentleman.

But this wasn't his 'end game', as he put it. In Tate's social media biographies, he described himself as an Entrepreneur. *Tate,* one read. *30. Entrepreneur. Fearless Adventurer. Manly Arts. To the Victor Go the Spoils.* His feeds were filled with staged photographs: Tate at a music festival wearing a feathered headdress, his abdomen striped with paint. Tate at a polo match, his white jeans rolled up above his boat shoes. Tate in ferocious sunshine at a motorsport event, wearing a bandana and brandishing a champagne gun – a thing that resembled an assault rifle, loaded with a bottle of Moët or Veuve Clicquot.

We met because I was a teller at the bank where he held his accounts and where he had tried to secure a loan to launch his entrepreneurial venture. I'd seen the application. He called himself The Charisma Coach. Charisma, he'd written, is a skill. It can be learned. Anyone can be charming. Anyone can be popular. Anyone can move through the world with grace and ease.

The loan was rejected, and so Tate started the venture by maxing out his credit cards. His efforts at building his business had continued throughout our relationship. Even in the new house, he set up a home studio with lights and a camera in a little storage room off the kitchen. He spent his days at work and his evenings against a plain white sheet he'd pinned to the wall, talking into the camera about expansive body language, phrases to instantly make people trust you, how to spot a liar, how to spot a narcissist.

He filmed himself from the waist up. He said this was because studies had proven that videos shot from this angle received the greatest amount of engagement. But I suspected that it was actually because of his legs. Tate never admitted this, but he hated his legs. He was built like a griffin, with a long neck and broad chest above the slight pudge of his abdomen, his top half promising a length his legs did not deliver. He was the only man I'd ever seen with cankles.

He was a clever dresser, though. In winter, with coats and trousers, you could almost fail to notice this quirk of his proportions. This is why I lived for the summertime. I'd buy him shorts in a variety of garish colours and patterns – pineapples, flamingoes, popsicles. When he wore them I loved to walk behind him; I was hypnotised by his mismatched halves. I found it oddly moving to witness the involuntary sway of his hips as his body tried, over and over, to put itself right.

Merry and Bruce, our next-door neighbours, came over while I was kneeling in the front garden one summer afternoon pulling out weeds. Or at least, I was pulling out what I thought were weeds. I'd never had a garden before, and I had to guess by sight, by leaf shape and colour, who was welcome and who was not.

Bruce wore clothes to suggest he could handle himself in the outdoors: cargo pants that could be zipped off at the knee, an old, lemon-yellow polo shirt with the collar turned up, a floppy khaki hat. Merry wore a zebra-print pussy-bow blouse and leather pants, despite the heat, the humid air. His shoes were hiking boots and hers were black pumps with a gold trim around the heels.

Merry came through the gate smiling and clutching a biscuit tin. Her hair was in soft feathery layers and her pink lipstick was dark and metallic. She looked wealthy, but she looked like a wealthy woman living in 1994.

'It's the welcome wagon!' she said. 'I brought shortbreads.'

I sat up.

'Bad time to be planting,' Bruce said.

I stood, slipped off my gloves, shook Bruce's hand, accepted a heavy, Chanel No. 5 kiss from Merry. Tate appeared, introductions were made, and before I knew it they were in the hallway. They were so glad to meet us, finally, Merry said. They'd been away at their beach house.

'You fish?' said Bruce.

'I've always wanted to learn,' said Tate.

'Every man should know how to fish,' Bruce said.

They continued into the house, Bruce knocking on the walls and Merry remarking on how clean everything was. 'Neat as a pin,' she said.

'It's so different now,' said Merry. 'I mean —'

'Good idea to paint the walls white,' said Bruce. 'Makes a small place like this look bigger.'

We went into the kitchen, then through to the dining room. I returned to the kitchen, conscious of the mud on my knees, and made coffee in a French press. I arranged the shortbreads on a plate decorated with rosebuds. It matched our coffee mugs.

The body had been found in the kitchen. The woman had been stabbed twenty-two times. Whenever I considered this fact, I couldn't help but think of what the judge handing down the sentence had pointed out: that this was many more times than was necessary to kill her. If killing her had been the murderer's sole intention.

'Nice table,' said Bruce when I brought in the coffee. He slid his hands along the edge, his wedding ring scraping the varnish.

'It's an heirloom,' said Tate. 'It was Alice's grandmother's. Had it sent over from England.'

'A good solid piece,' Bruce said. He pushed it a little, to test his assertion. It didn't move.

I poured the coffee, sat.

Merry took her mug and clucked at it fondly. 'Aren't these just darling,' she said.

She had a white pompom attached to the belt loop of her leather pants. I couldn't stop staring at it. The object was supposed to be a keychain, I think, but Merry seemed to be wearing it for purely decorative reasons.

Bruce broke the silence that had fallen.

'You like puzzles?' he said to Tate. 'Games?'

'Bruce loves games,' Merry said. I realised she'd crumbled her biscuit into dust on her saucer. I thought with anticipatory pleasure of shutting the door behind her and switching on the dust buster.

'I love games,' said Tate. He leaned forward, made eye contact. 'What do you play?'

'Oh, a bit of everything,' Bruce said, coy all of a sudden. He licked his finger and stuck it to his chest, where crumbs adhered to his fingertip. He ate them, then used his fingers to number off his areas of expertise. 'Board games. Card games. Jigsaw puzzles. Murder mysteries. Strategy. War games.'

'He just loves games,' said Merry.

'Do you play?' I asked her.

'Oh, I'm no good,' she said. Her lipstick was printed on the coffee mug; in the print I could see the squished ridges of her lips. 'Bruce is always looking for someone to play with. But it all goes straight over my head!'

'No use playing with women,' Bruce said.

'Well, I'd love to play sometime,' said Tate.

'Don't make that offer lightly,' said Bruce. 'You should know: I'm undefeated.'

'In what?' asked Tate.

'In everything,' said Bruce. 'Undefeated.'

Tate nodded. 'That's very impressive.'

'You don't believe me?'

Tate smiled, a hyena smile of self-abnegation.

'Of course I believe you. I'm just impressed.'

'You want a game now?'

Tate laughed. Merry laughed.

'I'm serious,' said Bruce.

Soon we stood in Merry and Bruce's house, admiring Bruce's selection of games. He had not been exaggerating. In the library – they had a library – the only books were those Bruce thought worth possessing: a single shelf of biographies and histories relating to the two world wars.

Everything else was games. There were games lined up on shelves, games in glass-fronted cabinets, and a long conference table on which sat a completed jigsaw puzzle of Monet's water-lilies. Bruce explained that he planned to spray it with adhesive and have it framed. He then went to a locked wooden cabinet and opened it, revealing stacks of other framed, completed puzzles. I saw the pyramids, a William Morris print, and ironically, a puzzle that showed the long corridors of a library, the shelves filled with red- and bottle-green gilt-edged books.

Bruce lifted up a frame that held a huge puzzle showing an assortment of overlapping Dalmatians.

'This is the hardest puzzle ever made,' he said.

He inhaled deeply, as if smelling his own success, while I looked into the sad dark eyes of the dogs.

'Well, my boy,' said Bruce, putting away the puzzles, closing the cupboard and turning the key in the lock. 'What's your pleasure?'

I saw the genuine excitement on Tate's face. I was embarrassed for him. He had a habit of getting swept up in other people's enthusiasms.

An example: a particularly wealthy client had once described to Tate the healing benefits of dog saliva. He said dog saliva contained a unique bactericidal composition which, as a healing agent, was unparalleled. This man had a rottweiler named Wagner. Wagner was encouraged to lick any cuts or abrasions his owner suffered. But it didn't stop there. Because this man believed that the dog was perpetually trying to optimise his wellbeing, he allowed Wagner to lick him wherever he liked, whenever he liked. He thus was able, he claimed, to absorb the full benefits of dog saliva, including its ideal pH, the proteins and nitrites it contained, and most importantly its ability to manage human body weight through the presence of *Lactobacillus reuteri*, which upregulated oxytocin levels.

Tate had relayed all of this to me. I was not sufficiently impressed.

'You don't understand,' he said. 'This guy does no exercise. He eats what he wants. But his abs are diamond-cut.'

'Sounds kind of crazy to me.'

'You haven't seen his abs.'

We couldn't have a dog in our apartment, but after that Tate went out of his way to visit our dog-owning friends at home. He would allow Beau and Shadow and Lurch to crawl all over him, licking his face and toes and hands, behind his knees. He would then step on the scales at home, watching to see if the miracle had occurred.

Merry, I realised, was tugging my sleeve.

'Best we leave them to it,' she said. She gave a conspiratorial little expression, wriggling her eyebrows in a way that made a strange feeling crawl down my spine. 'Secret men's business,' she added.

We went into the kitchen and sat on stools at the marble-topped island. Merry poured out two large glasses of chardonnay. She asked me if I'd like ice.

'No thanks,' I said.

She dropped a cube into her own glass. I heard the plop and crackle. I saw it start to melt, saw the icy water scribbling paths through the oily, viscous wine.

I felt an illicit thrill in drinking so liberally. Tate rarely drank, as he considered it a social crutch. Now, for me, it was a rare treat, something I looked forward to when he was out of town for work or dining with a client. I would buy a bottle of wine or a bottle of vodka, or both, and get slowly, extravagantly drunk on the couch or the bed or in the bath – sometimes all three. I would watch reality television and eat empty calories and let the unproductive hours roll away out of sight.

Very occasionally, I'd take a nip of vodka from a bottle I kept hidden in a kitchen cupboard. It was easy to hide; the bottle itself was a tourist souvenir my grandmother had brought back from her visit to Lourdes. It was translucent plastic in the shape of the Virgin Mary, wearing a blue plastic crown. The bottle was comically large; my grandmother sensed – correctly – that she would never visit Lourdes again, and so had opted for a jumbo, one-litre Mary filled with holy water.

'This will see me out,' she'd said.

She left the bottle to me, having used none of the water.

When I decided to use Mary to hide my vodka, I went to pour the holy water down the sink. But then, hit by a pang of guilt, and a vague fear of the Holy Spirit, I poured it into a snaplock bag and put it in the freezer instead.

I took another sip of my chardonnay. There was a clunk and a groan from the closed room where Tate and Bruce were playing.

'It's started,' Merry said. She drained her glass, letting the ice cube fall against her front teeth.

We sat in silence for a moment.

'How are you finding it? The house?' Merry asked. She topped up both our glasses, though mine was almost full.

'We're settling in.'

'You're happy?'

'We're happy.'

Merry licked her lips. 'You could always remodel,' she said. 'Here. Let me show you something.'

She hopped off her perch and clacked away until the carpet in the living room silenced her footsteps. When she returned it was with an armful of magazines. *Home Beautiful*, *Vogue Living*, *Belle*. They were old editions, the pages furred at the edges.

Merry fanned them out on the marble. 'Cushions make such a difference,' she said, licking her finger and opening one of the magazines. 'Don't you think?'

'I hadn't realised.'

'And throws. As long as they're neutral. How do you feel about ecru?'

I didn't have any strong feelings about ecru. But I said, 'I like it.'

'Me too,' said Merry. 'So soothing.'

She picked up another magazine and flipped through, finding a page.

'This is when we were famous,' Merry said.

It was a story about Merry and Bruce's house, its clever use of a natural palette, its chic, city-meets-country aesthetic. There was a photo of the library, when it still contained books. In another photo, Merry was lying suggestively on the very marble island where we now sat; she was propping up her head with her hand like she was lying on a grand piano in a lounge bar. Bruce stood behind her with his hands in his pockets. The article described him as *suave*.

'Wow,' I said.

'I'm just saying,' Merry said. 'If you ever want any advice.'

'I'd love your advice,' I said, smiling, using the open body language I'd learned from Tate. I too could be charming. I too could be popular.

Merry put her hand over my hand. Her nails were french-tipped. Her palm was sweaty. Even her bracelet was warm. I imagined her legs inside those leather pants, sweat dripping into her pumps.

'Have you ever thought about getting bangs?' she said. 'I think bangs would look great on you.'

'I think about it all the time,' I said.

She leaned forward, grabbed a hank of my hair, folded it up and held it against my forehead. She made her face studious.

'You should definitely get bangs,' she said.

I decided to try drinking my wine the way Merry drank hers. Instead of taking a sip, making my mouth small to restrict the flow, I opened wide and took a long, large swallow. My mouth felt coated, honeyed, redolent; in a few moments my mind was pleasantly fuzzy, my thoughts kinder, my body soft.

That evening I went home well before Tate and Bruce emerged from the library. I stumbled in, drunker than I realised, and fell asleep on top of the bedclothes, my espadrilled feet hanging off the end of the bed. At some point during the night, the heat still oppressive, Tate came in and collapsed next to me, shirtless but still in his flamingo shorts. His body was too hot to touch; heat radiated off him as though he was a brick that had been placed in a fire.

'What time is it?' I whispered.

And when there was no answer: 'Did you win?'

Tate said nothing for so long I thought he was asleep. Then I heard his voice.

'I think Bruce might be a genius,' he said.

For weeks afterwards I kept hearing about Bruce. Tate would huddle over a book Bruce had recommended, usually about military tactics, with occasional forays into personal finance. He'd look up game stratagems online and take copious notes. I heard fragments of Bruce's wisdom: Bruce says investing is like swatting flies. Bruce says game-play is vital, because it sharpens a man's instincts. Bruce says a good brandy will evaporate in the mouth. Tate often wandered home drunk; as far as I could tell, he hadn't told Bruce that he thought alcohol was a social crutch.

I didn't mind. I also didn't mind how much time Tate was spending with Bruce. I liked the silence, the stillness of being alone behind my new high fence. Besides, it gave me time to continue my own project, which was to find out all I could about the woman who'd been murdered in my house.

Tate and I had agreed not to do this. Tate said it was because he worried I would be too disturbed by the details, that I wouldn't be able to relax in our new home. The less I knew, he said, the better.

I'd accepted this. I liked Tate's habit of telling me things about myself that I didn't necessarily sense were true. It made me feel like liquid being poured into a vessel, taking on its form.

I looked up details of the murdered woman's life the way someone might look up pornography – careful to hide my digital tracks in the rudimentary way I knew how, and keeping one ear cocked for the key turning in the lock.

What I wanted was not the grisly details of the murder itself, or to know about the murderer. Those were the easiest things to find, dissected at length in the newspapers and by various squabbling bands of hobbyists online. What I wanted was information about the victim. I wanted to know all I could about the woman who might still choose to haunt me.

Her name was Bellinda, with two 'l's. She had dark hair, a tan, blocky eyebrows. Her last holiday had been to Greece; I found a photo of her squinting into the sun, accompanied by a plate of grilled octopus tentacles. She had been the proprietor of a bridal boutique called One Fine Day, and I was surprised to learn that the business still existed.

One Saturday, while Tate was with Bruce, I made an appointment at the store. On the phone they asked me the date of the wedding; unprepared, I gave them the date of my real wedding – April 6th.

'That's very soon!' the woman said.

'Sorry,' I said. 'I meant April 6th next year.'

'Oh good,' she said, relieved. 'You nearly gave me a heart attack.'

I spoke to the same woman when I went into the boutique: a place with tall mirrors, chandeliers, soft music, apricot-coloured carpet, and racks stuffed with lace and tulle, silk satin, beading, organza, bustles and trains.

'Have you brought anyone?' she said. 'Mum, bridesmaids … ?'

'I'd prefer to choose alone,' I said.

'Good for you,' said the woman. She'd gelled her hair into a low ponytail, and her scrunchie was black velvet. 'I like a woman who knows her own mind.'

She gave me champagne in a tall glass.

I told her I was marrying a very successful entrepreneur, and that I wanted to feel like a princess. I said I thought my husband was a genius. She asked me what kind of white I preferred – ivory? oyster? champagne? – then plucked a number of gowns from the racks. She hauled them into place around my body, making them fit using a series of giant clamps along my back. She complimented the lack of sun damage on my chest and shoulders.

'You have beautiful things here,' I said, rotating slowly on the apricot-carpeted podium. The mirrors were positioned so that I could see myself from all angles.

'You look gorgeous,' the woman said.

For a moment we both stood in silence, admiring my reflection.

'Do you have a favourite?' she asked.

I told her I needed time to decide.

'Ah,' she said, a little sadly. 'Usually a woman knows when she's found her dress. She knows the moment she puts it on.'

She gave me her card. On the back she'd written out the names of all the dresses I'd tried on: Arabella, Charlotte, Veronica, Monique.

'Do you like ice skating?'

Tate had asked me this at my teller window one day, his hand positioned in such a way that if I activated the security screen, his fingers would be chopped off. He didn't know yet that his loan application would be rejected.

'I don't know,' I said. 'I've never been.'

'Do you think you might?'

'I might.'

'You know, you look like you could be an ice dancer.'

'I do?'

'Yeah. You have poise.'

He must have thought I practised my poise. I'm not too proud to admit I enjoyed the flattery. I'd never wondered about my own elegance before. To find that I had it, that I was exuding self-possession somehow – that was a nice thing.

'I'm a great ice skater,' he said. 'I know a little rink, not far from here.'

'Oh?'

'Yeah. I go every Tuesday.'

'Today's Tuesday.'

'So it is,' he said.

Maybe Tate was charismatic. After all, I did go ice skating, even though I hadn't meant to, was wary of the process, wasn't dressed for it. There were things I liked about the rink. The cold, for one, and the way they pumped tinny versions of Russian classical music through the speakers. I liked the decals of snowflakes, how imperfectly they'd been applied, with bubbles visible between the sticker and the glass.

When Tate told me to let go of the rail, I did. 'Trust me,' he said. He took my hand.

Then, out of nowhere, a teenager – some boy in a flapping, heavy-metal T-shirt – came hurtling towards us. He called out, 'Incoming!' when it was too late. He knocked my hip; I landed splayed on the ice, and before I knew it someone's skate had run onto my hand. I looked down and saw fat drops of black-red blood spilling on the ice.

'Oh my god. Are you okay?' Tate swivelled up to me, his balance perfect. He knelt, and with the help of another man helped me to my feet and off the ice, blood slipping warm down my sleeve.

When we were seated on the blue plastic chairs in their bolted-on rows, he inspected my hand.

'I think you'll need stitches. It's pretty nasty,' he said. 'Does it hurt?'

'It's worse than it looks.'

'You mean – it's not as bad as it looks?'

No.

'Yes,' I said.

He smiled at that.

'See what I mean? Poise,' he said.

Later Tate would tell me that that was the moment he knew I was a woman of quality. I couldn't tell you when exactly he had let go of my hand, had manoeuvred his own body out of the way to safety, but I wasn't mad at him for that. It was too late to stop the accident. He couldn't have saved me. There was no reason to put himself at risk.

Late in the summer, Tate decided that it was time to invite Merry and Bruce to our house for dinner.

'What do you say?' he asked. 'You could make your famous turkey breast.'

He sat down at the kitchen table and started peeling an orange. Sometimes he'd peel an orange and not eat it. A clean peel was a manly skill, or so he'd heard, something that marked out a man of distinction. In seconds the orange was denuded, sitting pithy and undignified on the table. Tate threw the skin in the rubbish bin and left the orange where it sat.

I didn't have a famous turkey breast. It was Tate who liked turkey. He told me so early in our relationship. He said he liked it because it contained 29 grams of protein per 100 grams, and that the breast was also a rich source of niacin and vitamin B6. Soon after, he had come to my apartment. Bearing in mind his fondness for turkey, I roasted turkey legs and served them with a clotty cranberry sauce and mashed potatoes. I was pleased with how it had turned out, the turkey leaning fondly against the whipped blob of potato. If it didn't look like something you'd get at a restaurant, it at least looked like something you'd get in the ground-floor bistro of a three-and-a-half-star hotel.

Tate had smiled, eaten it, told me what a great cook I was.

It was only later that he confessed to me how much he'd struggled to eat that turkey leg.

'I felt really bad,' he said, hand on his heart. 'Truly. I just can't stand leg meat. Thigh meat. It tastes off to me. Know what I mean? Too …'

'Gamey?'

'Yeah.'

I'd assured him that I understood.

When Tate left the room, I ate the orange, easing out each of the segments and swallowing everything, flesh and juice and seeds, even all that bitter pith.

Without thinking, I asked the butcher for four turkey breasts. I had forgotten how monstrous a bird the turkey is. The butcher recognised my mistake; he said, 'You sure you want four?'

I hesitated.

'That's a lot of bird,' he said.

For some reason I felt compelled to commit to the error. My face grew hot. 'That's right,' I said. 'Four breasts.'

The shop had an old-fashioned scale with a needle that swung wildly as the meat was piled onto it. I paid, keeping my face impassive, and hauled the plastic bag home. When I unwrapped the breasts, I felt intimidated. I didn't want to be responsible for so many fibres, so much tissue. They felt heavy, chill, slimy; they slid across one another with a sensuousness that alarmed me. 'I hate turkey,' I whispered to no-one in particular. I rewrapped two of the breasts and slipped them into the freezer next to the snaplock bag of Lourdes water.

While I cleaned the house, Tate filmed one of his videos. It was about how to use the word 'but'. He was explaining how crucial it is to put 'but' in the right place. I could hear him making take after take. He said that all the emotional weight of a sentence occurs after the 'but'. If you're turning down an invitation, he said, you shouldn't say, 'I'd love to go, but I can't.' You should say, 'I can't go, but I would have loved to be there.'

It leaves the other party feeling good about the interaction.

This simple trick, Tate said, could revolutionise your life.

While mopping, I received a call from the bridal boutique. I made my voice nasal and said they had the wrong number. Then I hung up.

The call reminded me of Bellinda, of the ghost that had never shown itself. As I wrung out the mop, I felt my resentment grow. Then the thought occurred to me that perhaps the best way to ensure a haunting was to become a murderer myself. I didn't seriously entertain the thought – because who would I kill? Tate? My boss? A stranger on the street? – but it did make me wonder about my own capacity for murder. I looked at my hands, surveyed the knives in the kitchen. Would I be capable of it? Could I summon enough brute force to drive a knife between the fourth and fifth ribs? Did I have the strength in my hands to break someone's larynx?

I doubted it. After all, for much of my adolescence I had dreamed of being a nun. It began after a family trip to a small town where there wasn't much to look at. We drove to a museum that was housed in an old cloister. One of the rooms had been set up to look the way it did when inhabited by nuns. Cool, dove-grey stone, an iron-framed bed with starched white sheets, an enamel dish whose purpose was hinted at by its position, nosing out from beneath the bed. A little box on which the nun would kneel to pray. Rosary beads, a bible.

I remember the rush of desire I felt to be a nun on seeing that room. I could imagine my life so clearly: rising in the dark to pray, eating thin porridge, tucking up my habit in the front and back so I could do my share of household work, beating dust from carpets or hoeing the convent's vegetable garden. The whole enterprise seemed to me a wonderful cheat, a way to opt out of the hazards and obligations of adult life.

After that visit, I nurtured a secret fascination with nuns. I borrowed books about religious orders from the library, and used a box cutter to slice out pictures of them, which I pasted into a scrapbook.

My teenage reveries often centred around which order I would one day join. I didn't want to be a Poor Clare, because I had no interest in wearing brown. I preferred the habit of the Sisters of the Incarnate Word and Blessed Sacrament, its scarlet drama. I also liked the blue scapular and gold heart favoured by the Sisters of Mary Reparatrix. In my wildest dreams, I would imagine being a Daughter of Charity and wearing the full cornette, starching it into blanched architectural majesty every morning. For me, Vatican II was a grave disappointment. Nuns wearing tweed skirts and baggy turtlenecks, nuns in jeans – it was unthinkable. What was the point of being a nun if not to move through the world in such beautiful mystery, such privacy? To have your body be a total secret to everyone, even yourself?

My parents – despite my maternal grandmother's pilgrimage – weren't religious. So I never gave up on becoming a nun, not exactly; I just wasn't sure how it could be achieved. Preliminary enquiries revealed that I would need to be baptised, for one thing, and that after this there would be a series of other sacraments to complete before I could even consider taking vows. I didn't want to have to go to so much trouble. I just wanted someone to shave my head. I wanted to learn a little Latin, to eat my meals in silence, to possess no more and no less than the woman in the next room.

Was that so much to ask?

In my indecision I went with the current, got a degree, landed softly on an ergonomic chair behind a teller's window. I made that window my own little vestibule, wiping it down with hand sanitiser every morning, saying *Amen* in my head when the computer chimed to tell me it was ready to begin its work.

I chose my employer because their shirts were blue, the logo on the pocket red. With my first pay cheque I bought a little gold Tiffany heart pendant, which I wore hidden under my uniform.

I said a kind of rosary to Bellinda as I scrubbed and polished, then rinsed the turkey breasts and patted them dry. By the time the house was clean and the food prepared, dusk was falling. I could still hear the murmur of Tate's voice in the little room off the kitchen; I could hear his assurances, his confidential tone.

I ran myself a bath, adding no salts, no foam. It was too hot, like all of my baths. I liked to sit in the hottest bath I could stand. I would imagine steaming myself like a lobster. I would imagine how it would feel to be thrown like a martyr into a cauldron of boiling oil.

Eventually it got too much. I had to haul myself out and lie on the cold tiles, watching the steam rise from my body as though my spirit were leaving it. Then I heard Tate's knock on the door. 'Honey,' he said. 'They're here.'

Something about Merry's outfit made me want to embrace her. Not just because her sweater was pink and angora, but because it was shoulder-padded, with diamantes shooting out in a star-burst pattern from the collar. It was a sultry evening; I was in a floral dress, Tate in his popsicle shorts. Bruce wore the floppy khaki hat he'd had on when we first met, the kind you might wear fly-fishing. He didn't take it off inside. He wore the same lemon-yellow polo he usually wore, with the collar unbuttoned and turned up. His chest hair was grey and plentiful.

'Here,' said Merry. She pressed a bottle of chardonnay and a box of after-dinner mints into my hands. I passed them to Tate, hugged her lightly and took the opportunity to stroke the angora.

'Thank you,' I said. 'You shouldn't have.'

When they came into the hallway, Bruce sniffed. 'Bird?' he said.

'Turkey,' said Tate, smiling.

'I've always found it strange, men eating birds,' Bruce said. 'It's a woman's meat.'

'Turkeys have killed people,' I said.

'Only in the mating season,' said Bruce, maintaining eye contact. 'And even then they only attack people they perceive to be subordinates.'

Tate laughed. 'Guess you've got to get them before they get you,' he said.

I served the chardonnay with dinner. I served fresh rolls and green salad gently tossed with vinaigrette. I had made scrolls of the napkins, and every component of the main course was warm. I ignored most of the dinner conversation in favour of a serene survey of my own domestic competence. I was relieved and satisfied. I hadn't forgotten a thing.

Finally Bruce dabbed the corners of his mouth with his napkin and threw it over his empty plate.

'A good dinner,' he said. 'I'd give it a six out of ten.'

'Oh Bruce,' said Merry. Her cheeks were pink. The chardonnay was gone, as were two bottles of riesling Tate had chosen after careful consultation with the pimply yet sage attendant at the bottle shop. Everyone was a little louder, a little more at ease, the men spreading their legs and laying their arms along the backs of the chairs, Merry and I slathering melted butter on the rolls.

'Six is fair,' Bruce said, smiling. He was grabbing the edge of the table again. 'Generous even.' He looked at me. 'To tell you the truth, my dear, the turkey was a little dry.'

'You're a terror,' Merry said, opening another bottle Tate had fetched and filling her glass.

'I'll do better,' I said. 'Next time.'

Was I being sarcastic? I couldn't tell.

'Consistent basting,' said Bruce. 'That's what you need. Bird is finicky like that. Needs attention.'

He rose from the table. We all rose after him.

'How about a tour?' said Bruce. 'Settle the stomach before dessert.'

'Sure thing,' said Tate.

'You go ahead,' I said. 'I'll clear up.'

I made a ritual of it, of scraping and rinsing, of packing the dishwasher and hearing it commence its cycles. I looked up to the dark window above the sink, looked at the dark hollows of my eyes. They were sinking further into my head as I got older, that much was obvious.

I heard voices as our visitors moved around the house, opening doors, making remarks. I heard a heavy footstep directly above me. It could have been anyone's, but it was Bruce's foot I imagined, encased so securely in its hiking boot. The hairs on my arms went up. Is that you, Bellinda? I wondered. Are you trying to warn me?

But there was no answer.

I squeezed the sponge and set it down on the sink. Then I went to a cupboard, pulled out the jumbo Virgin Mary, removed her blue crown and took a nip of vodka.

'What's that? Holy water?'

I turned. Merry had struck a film star pose, leaning against the door jamb, hand on hip.

'Not exactly.'

She approached, picked up the bottle, sniffed it. 'May I join you? The men are talking about … men things.'

'Sure,' I said. I turned to fetch a glass, but when I turned back Merry was contentedly chugging vodka, leaving lipstick smeared on Mary's face. She had turned sassy, even a little flirty, now that she was drunk. I decided I liked her better this way. I took the Mary from her and chugged some vodka myself.

'You know, you're too pretty for him,' Merry said. She smelled like talcum powder, and like a baby goat. I supposed that was the angora.

'I could say the same to you,' I said.

Merry smiled, took another sip of vodka, picked up my dry hand with its chewed nails. 'I should take you to my nail girl,' she said. 'She'll change your life.'

'I'd love that,' I said, and in the moment, the vodka making my brain a drifting island in my skull, I meant it.

Merry poked the skin of my forearm with one of her long, glossy, french-tipped nails, and I felt an almost primal desire for my own nails to be glossy and french-tipped.

'See how strong they are?' Merry said.

'Like diamonds.'

'Exactly.'

That's when Bruce, and to a lesser extent Tate, filled the room.

'Finished the tour?' I said.

'What's in here?' said Bruce. He walked up to the tiny room off the kitchen where Tate did his filming. Without waiting for a reply, without waiting for permission, he pushed the door open. He took in the camera, the tripod, the wires snaking all over the floor, the white sheet tacked to the wall.

'You kidnapping people?' he said. 'Making ransom videos?'

'Not exactly,' said Tate. 'I —'

'You gonna cut some poor son of a bitch's head off?' Bruce said. He laughed. 'This some kind of Taliban deal, is that it?'

Tate smiled, and his smile was still so full of good faith. I wanted to warn him. If there were spirits in the house, I wanted them to warn him.

'It's for my business,' he said. 'I'm a —'

But Bruce didn't care what he was. 'Business?' he laughed. 'You?'

Tate folded his arms, then unfolded them.

'That's right,' he said. 'I studied enterpen … enrrepren … entrepreneurship,' he finally managed to say, his professional self trying to steer over his drunkenness. 'My idea is solid. I've researched the market.' And then, because he couldn't help himself, 'I got the highest score in my marketing class.'

'Good for you,' said Bruce.

Tate smiled again. 'I'd actually love to get your advice. Someday,' he said.

Bruce seemed so much more sober than Tate. He seemed so balanced, and to be surrounded by a magnetic field to which we were all drawn, little iron filings, all equally insignificant.

'You want my advice?' said Bruce.

He went to the kitchen bench. He picked up an after-dinner mint – I'd set them out on one of the rosebud plates, ready to take to the dining room – and peeled away a ribbon of gold foil to free the half-melted pastille inside.

'In all seriousness,' he said, 'I'd advise you to quit while you're ahead.'

Tate's smile was still there. He blinked. He didn't seem capable of processing what Bruce had just said.

'What?'

'Give up,' said Bruce.

I really wished Tate would stop smiling.

'What do you mean?' he said.

Bruce chewed the pastille and swallowed. He was in no hurry to reply. When he did, his voice was reasonable, even kindly.

'Look,' he said. 'You've done well for yourself. Decent job. Pretty wife. A nice house.'

He crumpled up the foil.

'What I'm trying to say is that business isn't for everyone. It's like singing, or football. You've either got it or you don't.'

'Coffee?' I said. I said it too quickly, too sharply, like I was trying to parry Bruce's blow – which I was – and like I knew it was already too late. Which I did.

To my amazement they stayed for coffee. And then sherry. At some point – my sense of time was getting hazy – we moved to the sitting room. Merry brought the Virgin Mary in and drank from it. I remember picking it up and being surprised to find it was empty. I remember Merry reaching out and stroking her nails through the length of my hair.

'Shiny,' she said.

All I really remember of Bruce and Tate's conversation is its ending. This came when Tate, slurry and boyish and shimmering with temporary confidence, looked at Bruce and said, 'How about an arm wrestle?'

Bruce chuckled, put his fists to his chest. 'Challenging the silverback, eh?'

'Why not?' said Tate. 'What do you have to lose?'

Bruce laughed, a real laugh filled with genuine mirth. He turned to me. 'Are you hearing this?' he said. He looked at me for a moment too long. Then he turned back to Tate and shook his head. 'You should count your blessings, buddy,' he said.

'What does that mean?'

'It means,' said Bruce slowly, clearly, 'it means that your missus can't cook for shit but she's a looker. Isn't that right, sweetheart?'

He turned to Merry, but Merry was asleep, her head against the couch, her mouth open, her breathing audible.

When Bruce turned back, Tate was kneeling on one side of the coffee table. He had taken a cushion to kneel on, and placed another on the opposite side. This attention to detail gave me a pang of guilt, of grief. The point of Tate's elbow was on the table.

'I'm serious, old man,' he said. 'We can settle this right here, right now.'

'There's nothing to settle,' Bruce said.

He stood up then, leaving Tate with his arm poised for battle. He went to the couch and picked Merry up and carried her, head dangling, down the hallway. He seemed competent in his movements, even sober, until he was passing the entrance of the room closest to the front door. There, Merry's head connected with the architrave and she woke. Thc noise she made was guttural, an *oof.*

Bruce paused. Merry had her eyes squeezed shut.

'Let me down,' she said.

'We need to get you home,' Bruce said. 'You've disgraced yourself again.' He said this in a fond tone, as though Merry's regular states of disgrace were an established component of their intimacy.

He went to keep walking, but Merry's hand – her french-tipped nails – dug into his arm.

'No, let me down,' she said. 'I feel sick. I'm going to be sick!'

Swiftly he put her down and stepped away, towards the front door. Merry clutched at the architrave with both hands, her forehead pressed against it, eyes closed. She looked like she was clinging onto a sinking ship.

I'll never be certain that I heard her say what I thought she said. What I heard was, in a mumble, 'Who could live here?' though it could also have been, 'Do I live here?' or maybe even, 'I'm going to be sick here.'

'What?' I said.

Merry didn't answer. She was sick. It rushed out, and I saw it all, scattered like runes: the wine, the turkey, the viscous brown streaks that I assumed were coffee or after-dinner mints. It piled up on the carpet. It splattered against the door, the architraves, against the hall table and onto the fresh white walls. Merry took a few deep breaths. Then she vomited again, a kind of afterbirth of vomit. She wiped her mouth with the back of her hand.

'I feel better,' she announced.

'Let me get you something for your head,' I said. 'Some ice.'

But when I came back with the only ice I'd been able to find – the snaplock bag full of holy water – Bruce had already walked Merry outside.

Tate and I stood in the hallway for a moment, sobered a little by the stench of vomit.

'What do we do?' said Tate. He ran his hands through his hair. 'It's everywhere.'

I sent him to bed. He took the bag of ice.

The first effort I made to clean up – my hair loose, feet tangled in my long floral dress – was less than helpful. It amounted, more or less, to taking some towels from the bathroom – the nice fluffy towels, I was drunk – and casting them gently over the scene.

It was only the next morning, with rubber gloves, a headscarf, and a bucket and scrubbing brush that I really set to work on the mess Merry had left. I made the water as hot as I could and it scalded me even through the gloves. I scrubbed the carpet, and the walls, and was amazed at how well things came up; by the time I was finished and everything had dried, the only way you would have been able to spot the stains was if you knew they were there in the first place.

The smell, though. The smell was another matter. We used everything we could think of: bicarbonate of soda and vinegar, lemon juice, odour-killing drops, tea-tree oil. We managed to expel most of it, but when you opened the front door, especially when the weather was warm, there was for years after a slight acrid smell, and the slight nausea that accompanied it.

I never mentioned this to Merry. And she never said a word about it the many times she came to visit after that night. Soon my nails were long and french-tipped. Soon I had bangs. Soon Tate packed away his sheet, his camera. And whenever I come into my house alone, I make sure to take a deep breath right in the place where the smell was the worst. A private thing, like a prayer, like a confession. If there are any spirits in this house, I hope it makes them happy. Or at least, I hope it keeps them from hurting us; I hope it's enough to stop our good luck from running out.

Future Moon

If you are reading this, you have twenty-eight days to tell twenty-eight people my story. Or else.

Or else what? you say.

Or else I will find you, and you will join me at the bottom of the well.

That is my story: they pushed me down a well.

I've had a lot of time to think since I've been here. I look up and see a disc of sky, blue all day and black all night.

Didn't you call out? I hear you ask. *Didn't you scream?*

Yes, and yes. But there was only the moon to hear me.

Did you know that she pulls everything on earth towards herself? In that way, a well is like a moon and now I am like a well. Look at my endless capacity. Everyone is welcome.

Or else what? A good question. I'm glad you're not afraid. I like to think that when I find you, asleep, your face will be relaxed, round and open as the face of the moon.

My mother told me once that the moon is retreating from the earth. Only by a few centimetres each year. But one day the tides won't be so strong. One day, a girl at the bottom of a well will hardly be able to see the moon at all.

For now, there she is. We reach for her and she reaches for us. But each day her grip lessens. In six hundred million years, she will have almost let us go.

Break Character

The Hair

Tom wasn't supposed to bring the wig home; it was peeled from his scalp like a banana skin every night. Then it was arranged on a faceless polystyrene head that lived in front of his dressing-room mirror.

I guess I shouldn't really call it a wig. The first time I saw it – the only time he let me come backstage – I said, 'That's quite a wig,' expecting him to laugh. He didn't. His makeup artist then explained, straight-faced, that theatre people didn't say *wig*. They said *hair*. *Where's your hair?* As though to claim it was the real thing would turn it into the real thing.

I wondered how The Hair had managed to make it as far as our third-storey apartment. Had he smuggled it out in a pocket? Had he left it attached to his head? That, I thought, was a possibility, given how he'd been lately, silent and brooding, an intense, glazed look in his eye. He wouldn't want to be separated from The Hair. He would have left it on until the sticky heat, the itch of it, forced him to tear it off.

Now, though, he was sleeping. I looked at the wig, bunched up on the bedside table like a frightened hamster. I reached out, tentative, as though it might flinch away from my hand.

I crept to the hallway and looked into the mirror, tried to scowl the way Tom scowled when eight p.m. struck and it was time to stride onstage as Alexandre Boulet. I'd seen it, just that one time I'd been allowed to see, how he left the dressing room with a sword in his belt and tall boots, glancing at himself in the mirror, his eyes lined, his face powdered, the place smelling of talc and cold cream and costumes that had been sweated in so intensely and with such regularity that the stains never quite came out.

I tried to sit the wig on my head. When the wardrobe assistants attached it to Tom's, they first used something called Gafquat, which stank and slicked his own hair flat as an otter's. No seam was visible between The Hair's edge and his skin. On me, it just sat there – inert, lopsided, almost embarrassed.

I slipped it off, and settled for burying my face in it, smelling the smell that was his and no-one else's.

The Labradors

Before Alexandre Boulet – before I found myself living with a man who ate only bloody steak, stale bread and hard cheese, limes, salted fish (no fruit, no vegetables), who drank beer and cider and wine but not orange juice or milk, who wouldn't touch a phone or a computer, who almost never washed his hands – I lived with a man known for being cast in commercials with dogs. Specifically, labradors.

Often the ads were for dog food (Tom throwing a frisbee, Tom rolling in the grass, Tom snoozing on a couch with a dog at his feet). Once, it was for a cologne called Pine Mist. Once it was for a weight-loss meal-replacement shake. Tom brought home some free samples he'd received on set and I threw them back at him.

For one of these shoots I came along. It was an open set. I watched as they filmed him walking along with a blonde labrador, throwing a stick, retrieving it from the dog's mouth, then throwing it again. When the stick became too wet and slimy, a gloved assistant would dash in and replace it with a fresh one; identical, pre-prepared sticks were stacked nearby.

A couple of hours in, the director said, 'You're doing great, Tom, but we're going to change up the dog. Something doesn't look right.'

I could have told them what the problem was. They looked too similar, Tom and the dog: same eyes, same hair, same wide open smile, the same joy in taking orders.

They replaced the labrador with a clever-eyed black and white collie, the type of dog who'd bite you just to see if she could get away with it.

Old-Fashioned

Tom used to work in a bar, an expensive one.

The night I met him, I was at that bar with a friend from work who had recently broken up with her fiancé. She was one of those people who seem to get drunk all at once; one moment she was fine, talking about the civil way in which they'd divided their books; the next she was casting her eyes cloudily around the bar for prospects, crying that she'd never find love again, striding off proud and unsteady to the restroom, and coming back with crooked lipstick and a train of toilet paper attached to one shoe.

'Aren't you cute,' she said to Tom, eating the olive from her martini. 'Buy me a drink?'

'I'd love to,' he said, 'but it's against the rules.'

She leaned forward and tried to touch his arm, but wound up stroking the rich mahogany of the bar instead.

Soon after, my friend departed, suddenly wide-eyed and aware in her drunkenness. She'd left Tom a handsome tip, which he pocketed in a single smooth gesture.

He turned to me.

'What are you drinking?' he asked.

Hall of Mirrors

'How old are you?' I asked.

He'd taken me to a carnival and was concentrating hard on a stick of candy floss, licking the sugar from his lips between bites.

'I'm seventeen to thirty-five,' he said.

Maintenance

I was eighteen.

'You'll thank me for this,' my mother said as we took our seats in front of the tall mirrors. 'Trust me.'

A succession of ladies then spent the next several hours 'fixing' me. They fixed my hair; they fixed my eyebrows, shaping them into lean arcs; they fixed my body hair, buttering each leg with hot pink wax. They fixed my faint moustache by sticking a needle into each follicle and electrocuting it until it was dead.

Then my mother poked my protruding belly with a long, painted nail.

'They can't fix this,' she said. 'This you'll have to manage on your own.'

I haven't had a moustache since. But sometimes I catch myself staring out my office window, stroking the place where it would have been.

The Arrival of Alexandre Boulet

Before Tom got the part, I'd never heard of *The Pure White Light of Morning* – even though, as everyone kept telling me, it was a classic. An early nineteenth-century classic, over a thousand pages long, by the brooding genius Jean-Baptiste Dupont. I didn't read books like that. I'd majored in economics and then gone to business school. I didn't have time for melancholic sagas in which everyone gets to make a speech before they die.

One night, I was working in the living room when Tom walked in with the book under his arm. Usually he only read the sports section, or the reviews.

'What's that?'

'Nothing. It's for a part. An audition.'

'A film?'

'No, it's a show.'

He passed me the book; there was an illustration of crossed, tasselled swords on the cover.

'*A timeless tale of rebellion and romance*,' I read.

'What do you think? Could I play period?'

They'll have to dirty up those teeth, I thought.

'Sure,' I said. 'What's the part?'

'Alexandre Boulet,' he said, in a mock-grave voice which was deeper than his own. 'A nineteenth-century war hero, struck down by poverty on his return to Paris. In desperation he turns to crime, and becomes captain of a gang of charismatic thieves, Les Sangsues. Which means The Leeches. In French.'

'Oh?'

'Of course, he only breaks the law to save the love of his life, Mathilde.'

'That's nice,' I said, and went back to work, my hands blued by the glow from my laptop.

'Don't you want to know how it ends?'

I looked up, smiled tiredly. I had work to do.

'They die?'

Tom frowned. 'It's very moving,' he said.

Then he took the book into the bedroom, and closed the door.

I Wouldn't Do That, If I Were You

One day, getting dressed, I bent over to slip my foot into a pair of pantyhose.

Then I registered an odd feeling – I was being touched, but not in one of the usual places. The approved places.

I looked down. Still lolling in bed, smiling, propped on one elbow, Tom was prodding the rolls of fat that hang from my abdomen.

They aren't big, but they're there.

He laughed. I think he expected me to laugh too.

At Least I Wasn't the Tree

When I was in grade two, I won a part without realising I was even auditioning. The drama teacher, Mr Koch, told everyone in my class to line up on the floor of the gym, kneeling on all fours. Then he told us to bark like dogs. He told us that the best, loudest, most convincing dog would win a prize.

So I barked. I barked and howled my classmates into submission.

The prize? A part in the grade six play.

For the dress rehearsal, Mr Koch affixed a dog hat made from scraps of brown carpet to my head; it had long floppy ears. Everyone around me laughed.

'You're so cute. Look at your cheeks!' said a blonde girl named Kimberley, pinching my face. She was dressed as a butterfly: pink pantyhose stretched over coathangers to make wings, glitter on her face and down her arms. She tugged on one of my dog ears and smiled, wrinkling her nose.

As I walked through the school gates that afternoon, a group of boys started barking at me.

When the time came to perform, I couldn't bring myself to bark at anything above a conversational level. Mr Koch lifted the hat from my head after the show. He'd been an actor too, once, and conveyed his disappointment without uttering a word.

The Heart-throb

Years before *The Pure White Light of Morning*, Tom was cast in a film called *The Heart-throb*; this was back when he was playing seventeen to thirty-five, rather than twenty-two to forty.

'It sounds awful,' I'd said. I was trying to read the newspaper, sitting on the living-room floor eating 99% fat-free yoghurt straight from the tub.

'Don't be so negative. It's fun. It'll *be* fun. Besides, my agent says it's a vehicle,' Tom said, coming up behind me, slipping his arms around my waist.

'Like a sedan?'

He tickled me and I yelped.

'What're you reading about?' he asked, staring down at the columns of numbers.

'Stocks.'

'They up or down?'

'Both.'

'Huh,' he said.

The Heart-throb went straight to DVD. The DVD didn't sell well. I patted Tom's shoulder and told him it didn't matter, but all the while I couldn't help but imagine the leftover copies being destroyed, all those images of Tom – the blond hair, the big white teeth – slowly consumed by fire.

I Wouldn't Do That, If I Were You (2)

It was a windy night; a branch kept slapping our window like an open palm. *White Light* had been running for two weeks; Tom had been receiving the first good reviews – glowing reviews – of his life.

We'd been out. Tom looked like Tom but at dinner he ate a chicken leg with his hands, ignoring the enquiring glances of other diners.

When we arrived back home, he let me open the door, then kissed me in the cold hallway; a hard and urgent kiss. He lifted me by the hips and pressed me into the wall, causing the top of my head to flick the light switch. The room was flooded with light, and we were left looking at each other in full colour while the tungsten hummed passively on.

Signature

People started asking Tom for his autograph.

He had prepared for this; one evening, I came home to find him sitting in his underwear at the kitchen table, pens scattered everywhere, practising his signature.

'I've got it down to three,' he said. 'Which one do you like?'

I set down my briefcase, tried not to stare at the pen marks on the table.

'That one,' I said, pointing to the one that most resembled his real signature.

'Huh,' he said. Then he turned to smell my chest. 'You smell good,' he said. 'What is that?'

'L'Autre,' I said.

I'd gone into a perfumerie, a tiny, exclusive boutique, and asked for something that would linger in a room after I'd left it. Something people would remember.

L'Autre was the perfume the matron in a black pantsuit had produced.

'What *is* that?' my mother asked when I met her for lunch later that day.

She leaned forward, blowing smoke out of her nose before inhaling my wrist like a sniffer dog hunting for contraband.

'Bah.' Her head jerked up. 'Smells like BO. Men will hate it.'

Now, in the mornings, I step out of the shower, spray L'Autre in a cloud above my head and walk into it, my eyes closed, letting its tenacious little atoms grip my hair and clothes and skin.

Night Is the Only Home I Know

It's his classic line, the one Boulet says before he commits the final crime, the one that sees him executed by a firing squad. *Night is the only home I know.*

Alexandre says it to the woman he loves, Mathilde.

During rehearsals Tom took to saying the line to himself, dozens, hundreds of times per day; *Night* is the only home I know; Night is the *only* home I know; Night is the only *home* I know.

He said it into the mirror. He said it in the shower. He said it reading the sports section and again when watching TV.

He'd get up in the night when he thought I was asleep and pad around the living room, saying it again and again, until he must have been numb to the words, to their meaning.

I asked him to say it for me, once. To me. 'Pretend I'm Mathilde.'

He looked shocked; he didn't say it. He didn't say anything, and I didn't ask again.

Allowances

On the first of every month I do a calculation, adjust the amount for inflation and cost-of-living increases.

Neither of us says a word about it.

Grooming

One night: my hand on his chest.

'Tom,' I said. 'Tom, you have chest hair!'

I looked closely at the little blond hairs, sparse but plucky, laying themselves flat against his skin.

'I've always had chest hair.'

'No you haven't.'

I pulled at them, watching the skin rise in little tents.

'I did. I've just been … removing it. Until now.'

'Removing it? Like waxing?'

'Exactly. Loads of actors do it.' He yawned. 'I'm growing it in for *White Light*. People didn't wax in the nineteenth century.'

'Maybe I'll stop waxing.' I nudged him, smiled, assumed a pose that would usually prompt him to say, 'Aren't you cute.'

He shrugged. 'If you like.'

He switched off the lamp.

I laid my head back on his chest, then grasped one of the newly sprouted hairs. When I yanked it out, he gasped.

The Heart-throb (2)

That film did have one fan. My mother. She tracked down a bulk lot of DVD copies on eBay for $4.99.

'There he is! The heart-throb!' she'd say to Tom when we visited. She'd then cuddle him vigorously until he found a way to eel out of her grip.

She liked to make us watch the film with her. She had, she told us, many favourite lines; she proved this by speaking along with Tom's character from start to finish.

'I'm a dreamer, Veronica. And I think you're a dreamer too,' said my mother, blowing smoke rings. 'You're with me in every word I say and every breath I take.'

She closed her eyes.

'Come with me, and we'll be the people we were always meant to be.'

Alexandre Boulet Must Die

'You should have warned me.'

'You could have read the book.'

'I know, I meant to, but – God, Tom, it's a little graphic, don't you think?'

I'd brought him flowers, a big bouquet of white blooms. ('Nothing too feminine,' I'd told the florist.) It was the night I saw The Hair, and we were back in his dressing room after the show. There were little explosions of blood all over his frilled shirt.

'Well,' he said. 'I'll be back to life tomorrow. And the next night. And for the Saturday matinee. I'm resurrected eight times a week.'

I didn't say anything else but wondered what it must be like, to run out of luck over and over; to make all the same choices, even though you know how it ends.

The Company of Monsters

Once, he said, he'd been in a show whose chorus was a company of monsters, all in different masks. Before each performance the actors took a mask from a hamper full of them. After the show all the masks were thrown back in. The smell, Tom said – the smell inside those masks. God it was awful. All that trapped breath from all those different bodies. A different face every night. And you never knew who you'd be, or who had been you the night before; or who, tonight, was inside the face that you would wear tomorrow.

Break Character

It was a Friday night. It had been a good day at work – sunny weather, happy clients. I was maybe a little drunk, after two or three vodka sodas. I'd had pizza on my own, on the couch, and was still there, in a tracksuit, waiting for him to come home.

He came in late, and wandered through the hallway straight into the darkened bedroom.

'Hey,' I called out. Then, louder, 'Hey. Tom!'

He didn't come out, so I followed him into the bedroom,

switched on the light. And there he was – not Tom, but Alexandre Boulet, tall, sweaty, pungent, determined. In full regalia.

He took a step back from me.

But I walked right up to him, took him by the waist.

'This is very convincing,' I said, whispering into the talcum and hairspray smell at his neck. 'Totally believable.'

A hand – a slow but insistent hand, was placed between my breasts and pushed slowly backwards, until I was as far away as his arm could reach.

There was a pause, a silence.

'Tom?'

His eyes weren't shining and wholesome anymore. They roiled like the sea.

'Tom? Where have you been?'

'Leave me,' he said.

'Tom – stop it. You're crazy. You're being crazy! Hey! Look at me!'

He looked. Stepped close, until there was almost no distance between us; looked through me, straight down at all the versions of me there were to see. Then he huffed once, flared his nostrils, and walked out the door.

The Labradors (2)

In bed one Sunday I was reading the newspaper and came across an article warning the owners of loveable family dogs to beware. Rottweilers and pit bulls might have the bad reputations, it said, but really it's golden retrievers and labradors who are the most lethal. Lethal because you think you know their limits but you don't; their violent outbursts are all the more terrible because they're delivered by that beatific face, that clean pink mouth, those teeth you paid a vet to polish up while the dog was sedated; dreaming, you thought, of your life together – of a quiet walk and a quiet meal, then curling up on the floor at your feet.

Animus

'There are two more pieces to go in,' Leonard said. 'They're a late addition. The owners took some convincing.'

Everything else for the exhibition was in place. It would open in a week. Before my shift began, I liked to wander among the treasure he'd amassed – the gilt frames, marble statues, parures glittering hyperactively against black velvet. I was always tempted to push over a vase, or pull out my keys and slash a canvas. I would imagine the scene in loving detail: the zipping sound of the painting as I bisected it, the shattered Sèvres littering the ground. Such were my daydreams.

Splendour: Contested Treasures was the name of the exhibition. The essay in the heavy catalogues – which were also expensive, with flocked covers and marbled endpapers – was full of words like *sumptuous*, *grandiosity*, and *luxuriant*. There was also *starvation*, *furious* and *bonfire*, but I suppose it's a question of emphasis. Everything in the exhibition had been stolen, or nearly destroyed, or hidden in an attic or tabernacle to keep it from looters. Displays of opulence, Leonard argued, led almost inevitably to envy, and then to violence.

I had known Leonard since art school. I knew that he truly frothed for beautiful things. Once, he'd spent the weekend in his parents' garage figuring out a way to gold-plate objects. He hooked a car battery up to a bucket filled with some toxic mixture of chemicals, then ran through the house like a high, skinny Midas, finding things – coins, paperclips, forks and spoons – to drop into the solution. 'I'm a motherfucking emperor,' he yelled, standing on a chair, brandishing a gold-plated coathanger.

Eventually there was an explosion. A piece of that mock gold melted right into Leonard's skin, above the outer corner of an eyebrow. 'One more inch,' he said later, 'and I'd have been blind.'

'Anyway,' he said, 'will you go?'

We were standing in his office.

'Can't you send the van?'

He shook his head. 'These are not van people,' he said. 'They're old. They're eccentric. They're suspicious of anything too official. They'll like your clapped-out Vauxhall – they'll find it authentic.'

He smiled his cajoling smile.

'All old money drives shit cars like yours, Tracey,' he said.

I flinched; I hate my name. He used to call me Trace. And he calls my car a Vauxhall, though he didn't visit London until he was twenty-five.

'Trust me,' he said. 'And take some flowers.'

After art school, I kept painting; he did a masters in curatorship. Now he curates and I stand in the corner of the gallery, among his arrangements, saying 'No flash photography' and watching people pick their noses and adjust their balls when they think they're alone.

I still paint. It's where my money goes: on pigments and canvas and brushes. The smell of turpentine still makes me giddy.

I paint nudes, mostly. But I can't afford models, and my friends with their slack, postpartum belly-skin and knee-folds are no longer willing subjects. They don't understand that this is what I want, what I'm greedy for – the brown splotches and spider veins and tough, thick toenails whitened with fungus. It's my dream to paint a close-up portrait of an anus, in satiny dark pinks and purples, with hints of sienna in the folds, and that black knowing pupil at the centre.

If I could get a good enough look at it, I'd paint my own.

In fact, I am my own subject most of the time. I crouch in my apartment, watching myself in the mirrors I've amassed over the years; round and square, bevelled and wood-framed, mould-speckled, acid-etched. Mirrors, and unsold paintings of myself as I gaze into them, are stacked against the white walls. I'm fanatical about those walls. I sponge them as gently as you would a lover's back, and annually I paint them white again.

Of course, it doesn't keep out the noise that filters through – dull fights, dull routine fucking on weeknights, the sound of supermarket bags hauled onto a counter, a news reporter's schooled concern. But it makes me feel clean.

On days I can't paint, I look at my old works. I stare into my own painted eyes, dark and suspicious. I can study the sag in my breast or the length of my inner thigh, smooth like the belly of a fish, for hours. Sometimes I paint myself with a cock instead of a cunt; a modest, workmanlike sort of member, nestled content on pert testes or cradled, erect, in the palm of my hand.

They are not, I have been told, commercial works.

'You've got something,' said the owner of my last gallery as she was letting me go. 'But can't you bring me a pretty girl, or at least a dog? Let's face it, Tracey, old pudenda doesn't sell.'

That night I'd sat on my tiny balcony among the dead plants, wearing a worn-out T-shirt and nothing else. I stroked the fur of my old pudenda, soothing her wounded pride. A man looked up from the street. I didn't close my legs. He dismissed me with a wave of his hand and moved on.

It was a beautiful drive, the hills a lush, near-toxic green in the late-spring heat. I wound the window down, listening to the radio lose reception, turning it up louder and louder as the static grew, voices punctuating it less and less frequently: *baby*, *why*, *love*, *your heart*, *I would die*. The wind whipped my hair into my face and I liked that too, the sting of it, the quivering lines across my vision as the road hurtled towards me.

The car had been my mother's, and like her its complaints were loud and frequent. But I loved it anyway. It was solid, heavy, reliable; I had no desire to trade it in for something new and flimsy, whose lifespan would be short by design.

Drive carefully, Leonard had said. And watch for roos – they're everywhere up there. I'd rolled my eyes. It was so like Leonard to think everyone was attempting to sabotage him, wildlife included.

The paintings' owners lived among beautiful hills. The house was built at the top of one, surrounded by rolling lawns and gardens that were obnoxiously successful. Along the drive were rosebushes groaning under their own gorgeous weight.

As I walked up to the house I twisted buds off with my fingertips.

The man who opened the door wore a jumper with a dribbled soup stain on the chest and corduroy trousers which had balded at the knee.

'Miss Aitken?'

And when I nodded: 'How do you do?'

'How do you do,' I answered. I love these little tests that the rich administer: *How are you?* they ask, waiting to see whether you'll say *good* instead of *well.*

I presented the spiny bunch of native flowers I'd brought, and the man poured me a gin and tonic.

'You look like an artist,' he said. 'Are you an artist? A painter?'

'Yes,' I said.

'What do you paint?'

My old pudenda. 'I'm mostly interested in the female form.'

'Aren't we all,' he said, casting a sly glance and pulling on his drink until he made a sucking noise like an emptying bathtub.

He offered to give me a tour and show me the other paintings in their possession. 'It's not really a collection,' he said. 'More of an accumulation.'

His wife joined us, in from the garden and smelling of fresh earth. Her grey bob knew not to touch her shoulders. She padded along in her gardening clothes, saying very little.

'Anyway,' the husband said, 'I suppose we should get down to business.'

We fetched the crates from my car, the wife watching from the verandah.

The paintings I would be taking were in the library. This was a high-ceilinged room, which could have been grand if they cared about grandeur. As it was, an elderly cat chewed determinedly at its claws on the rug, and the wife extended one foot, its cashmere sock drooping, to stroke the animal's head with her toes.

'Are those the paintings? On the desk?' I asked.

'Indeed. Our very own "contested treasures".'

'Mr Foster says it's a miracle they've survived,' I said.

Mr Foster was what I had to call Leonard in situations like this.

'Oh yes,' the man said. 'I'm not too fond of them – I find them a little vulgar, to tell you the truth – but our relatives on the continent managed to smuggle them to an aunt in New York. She died, and her son brought them here, and the family has dwindled, so I suppose they're ours now.

'What about you?' he said, and his smile showed the brown grout between his teeth. 'You're a painter. What do you make of them?'

It's strange seeing valuable works outside a gallery. No context, no hush, no-one to say don't touch, don't stand too close. The pair of paintings were of an artist and his wife. The artist had done well: a series of commissions had left him ruddy-cheeked and bursting out of his silver waistcoat. The wife smiled wanly. She leaned her chin on her hand; the dog at her feet was silky and idiotic.

'Very accomplished,' I said.

The man snorted. 'A little middle-class, though, wouldn't you say?'

He plunged his hands deep into his corduroy pockets and left them there as I arranged the paintings in their crates.

'I'm more of a landscape man, I suppose. Give me a sea crashing against some rocks, or at least a nice field. I'm partial to fields.'

'Still,' I said, 'they're excellent examples of the style.'

'Well. You're the expert,' he said.

I closed the crates and drew their bolts.

'When will we have them back?' he asked.

'As soon as the exhibition closes. We'll take good care of them,' I said. 'Will you be joining us for the opening?'

He'd found a morsel of food stored in his teeth and was grinding it up.

'Thank you, but no,' he said. 'I can't stand museums.'

As I crunched down the gravel drive, the old white not-Vauxhall creaking and bumping, I looked in the rear-view mirror and saw him wave, one arm around his wife. I envied him briefly, but then I took pleasure in such brief envious flashes – moments when I crawled into another skin and looked out at a world which was mine, a world I could possess.

I'd stayed too long at the old house. It was early evening and the light was fading. Crepuscular. A teacher had said that about my work once. 'It's neither day nor night in these paintings,' he said, and tapped his fingertip against the desk. 'But one of them is coming.'

I liked that teacher. Leonard and I had him for a drawing class. He'd told us to look at the models, to really look.

'I want to see that wart,' he'd say, as the model remained reclined and impassive. 'I want those silver snail-trails along her hips.'

One day he asked us to do an experiment. 'It's to test your temperaments as artists,' he said. 'First, draw a box. And then draw yourself inside it.'

He walked around the room, looking at each of our boxes in turn. To Leonard, he said nothing. When he saw my box he laughed and said, 'Oh Miss Aitken. I knew you wouldn't disappoint me.'

Later, Leonard reached out to snatch my sketchbook.

'What did you draw?' he asked when I pulled it away.

'Show me yours,' I said.

—

It was when I was coming over a rise that I gasped and went for the brakes. All I saw was movement. Here's the roo, I thought, and then, when I realised the shape was human: It's a ghost.

But it was neither. It was a hitchhiker, a young man in a ratty leather jacket with a rattier nylon backpack.

He ran up to the car and tapped on the passenger window, smiling with one side of his mouth. He was handsome, in a rough sort of way – lank, light brown hair; stubble; a deep, damaging tan. The intense, pale eyes of an addict. His clothes would have been nice, once. I could imagine the whole story: a ticking clock in the house where people were waiting for him, and on the mantelpiece, photos from another time: him young and fresh and limber, winning a race, or fishing with his father, or with an arm around his mother, her eyes closed in maternal bliss.

I leaned over and wound the window down. 'You scared me,' I said.

'Are you going to the city?' His eyes gleamed. This man could be a murderer, I thought.

'Yes,' I said.

'Could I get a lift?'

'What are you doing out here?'

He shrugged. 'I was with friends,' he said.

'Where are they?'

'Wish I knew. I woke up – they'd gone.'

'Some friends.'

'Right?' He laughed and his laugh was wheezy. 'Please,' he said. His mouth twitched.

I must have inclined my head; he took it for a nod. Before I knew it he was in the car, landing beside me in the passenger seat. He dropped the backpack between his knees. His odour was potent: smoke, dirty sneakers, and the mildew of clothes that haven't dried properly.

'Thanks, man,' he said. 'Most people won't even slow down. Most people are pricks.'

He let out a bark of laughter. My stomach tightened. He started to bob his knee up and down, then turned the dial on the radio until the static vanished.

We'd been driving for a while when I said, 'Where are you headed?'

'Just to the city,' he said. 'Drop me anywhere.'

His knee hadn't stopped bobbing. I could see how thin his thigh was, barely more than a femur. I found myself wondering what he looked like naked. I wondered whether I'd be able to see all his ribs, the knobs of his spine, whether his navel would be stretched and shallow, his sex obscenely fat compared with the rest of his body.

This thinness reminded me of my mother, who had insisted on dying at home. I suppose that's how she got me back there. I spent months living at that house, my days occupied by the little chains of nothing that take up time while you're waiting for someone to die. Pegging her nightdresses on the line and watching the wind fill them out in a way she no longer could. Poaching an egg with forensic concentration. Polishing my shoes, then her shoes, though she had no need of them.

I liked to watch her sleep. Even while dozing her expression was haughty. I could see her skull, the way her body was already dismantling itself.

When she died, finally, I wanted to keep her ring. They sawed it off for me, her knuckles having become monstrous with arthritis. I never had it repaired. I tied the broken thing to a length of fine chain, and still wear it around my neck, where the rough edges graze the skin of my breasts.

'Sorry, Mum,' I say out loud sometimes, though I'm not sure what I've done.

Mum had wanted me to marry Leonard.

'He'll be good for you,' she said, when she realised I was never going to stop painting and become a bank teller or a florist. 'You could have a nice life.'

Leonard has a nice life, I thought, imagining his housekeeper's hands picking over his freshly laundered Y-fronts, finding the ones that were old, bagging, losing elasticity, and throwing them in the bin.

Could I have woken up every morning smelling Leonard's sour breath, advising him about his hair, choosing his shirts, pretending to care about his little rivalries with other curators, other galleries? Maybe. Maybe that's what happiness looks like: balding, greying, stroking a cat with a foot clad in cashmere, dribbling soup down your chest.

The hitchhiker asked me for a cigarette.

'I don't smoke.'

'Oh,' he said. 'No worries.'

He started drumming his fingers on his legs, whistling tunelessly. The car in front of us was a huge black SUV with tinted windows, driving below the speed limit. I tapped the brakes.

'Sunday driver,' I said, stretching my fingers. It wasn't something I'd usually say. It was something my mother would say.

'Yeah. Fucken cunt,' the man said. He turned and looked at me. 'Sorry for the language.'

I shrugged. I told him it was all right.

He flipped down the sun visor and peered at his face in the mirror, then turned to look at the back seat.

'What're those?' he said.

'Oh nothing,' I said. 'Some paintings.'

'Paintings?' he said. 'Like … art?' He fluttered his hands in the air.

'Yep.'

'Are they yours?'

'You mean – did I paint them?'

He hesitated for a moment. 'Yeah. Did you?'

'No. The guy who painted them died a long time ago.'

'Is he famous?'

'Not famous. Well known, maybe.'

'Huh.'

'I paint too, though,' I said after a moment. 'I'm an artist.'

'Oh. That's cool,' he said. 'Are you famous? I mean, "well known"?'

'Not exactly.'

'Maybe once you're dead.'

I gave an awkward laugh.

'Maybe.' I glanced at him.

The SUV turned off the highway. I could accelerate again.

'I paint portraits,' I said. 'Studies of people.'

He was looking at his filthy fingernails. I felt a surge of boldness.

'I'd like to paint you.'

'Me?'

He looked up.

'Yeah. I think you'd make a great subject, actually. You've got good bones.'

He laughed his wheezy laugh, then balled his hands into fists and ran them up and down his thighs.

'Well? What do you say?'

'Dunno. Does it pay?'

'Call it payment for the ride.'

'Well,' he said, suddenly shy. 'I dunno. Maybe.'

And perhaps it was the promise in that 'maybe' that distracted me. I turned to look at his face, greedy to capture its angles, its damage. I never saw the roo coming.

Luckily, I only clipped it; its hind connected with the driver's side headlight, which immediately went dark. There was a thump and a moment of sickening slow motion as I felt the car veering onto the wrong side of the road, and then onto gravel. I braked, hard. The not-Vauxhall, old but solid, juddered to a halt.

'Fuck!' the young man shrieked. 'What the fuck was that?'

I left the car running, the keys in the ignition.

'It's all right,' I said. I spoke in some ersatz mother's voice which I hoped would calm the both of us. Smoke rose from the front of the car.

I got out and then he got out, running his hands through his hair.

'Fuck!' he said again.

I went to where the roo lay. I'd never been so close to one, never realised how long their claws are, how thick their tails. This one was snuffling, heaving, stinking in the way terrified animals do, as though stink is enough to deter a predator. I stayed at its back, unsure whether it would lash out at me.

'Shit,' I said. I sank to my knees.

I looked up at the boy, who came to stand next to me. 'We can't leave him like this.'

'What?'

'It would be cruel.'

I was fumbling with my phone in the twilight. I switched its torch on and ran the beam over the kangaroo's dusty dead-leaf coloured body, trying to find what was wrong. There was no visible injury, only the movement of muscle and bone beneath its pelt, the shallowness of its breath.

'What do you mean?' the boy said. He was shaking. He couldn't keep the panic from his voice.

'You know what I mean.'

I caught his face in the torch-beam. His eyes were wide. The skin on his face was taut. Yes, I thought. I'd love to paint you like this: vulnerable, pale with fright.

'How? You have a gun or something?'

'No.'

I leaned over the kangaroo, as far as I dared. I tried to speak in a soothing voice: 'There, now. There, there. It's okay.'

The boy's stink was as strong as the roo's.

'I would do it myself,' I said. 'But I don't have the strength. I'd make it worse.'

He paused, swallowed, looked down at his hands.

'Okay,' he said. 'Okay. I've got something in my backpack. I'll go get it.'

As his footsteps crunched behind me, I tried to imagine how it would feel, to move forcefully enough to snap bone. As though propelled by this thought, my hands moved to the animal's neck.

They were hovering above – they had not even touched it; the creature would barely have been able to sense my fingers at the edges of its fur. But it made a sound, a sort of terrible, revolted growl, and jerked itself heavily to its feet, the dirt and debris falling as it bounded away, bounded straight into the scrub as fast as it could.

Was I relieved or disappointed that the boy's resolve would not be tested? There was no time to consider; I heard the slam of the car door.

Soon gravel was spraying from under the tyres. I watched the car vanish, and I thought: This is what it's like to watch me drive away. I thought of my mother, peering through her window, dropping the curtain back in place after I was gone.

So there I was, in the near dark. No knife. No claws. Instead of a cock, my old pudenda. You have your phone, I thought. You could call Leonard. You could call the police.

I switched the phone off.

I could not muster up any unease at the thought that Leonard's paintings were gone. I imagined him finding out what had happened and turning red beneath his sparse blond hair. I imagined him trying to tell the old couple, trying to arrange the words.

I wondered whether the boy would risk selling them, or whether he'd hang them on the wall of whatever dank flophouse or squat he lived in. Perhaps he'd give them to his mother.

What I like to think happened is that he lit a cigarette and burned their eyes out, wife then husband. If I concentrate, I can smell the toxic smoulder of oil paint and varnish, hear the hiss as the thing is extinguished.

One night, a long time ago, I waited until Leonard was drunk and asleep in the bed we were sharing. He stank of whiskey and gilt. I picked up his sketchbook and flipped to the last page he'd used. There was his version of our teacher's test: a box, and a skinny Leonard in the lower left corner, making the space seem vast. I smiled.

My box? I'd filled it with a pillowy, marshmallowy rendering of my body, a body that looked as though it were still expanding and might never stop. I filled every corner. I thought I looked like a baby who'd stayed too long in the womb. A baby who'd open his eyes in there and realise he could be trapped forever; who'd grope downwards, trying to distinguish the limits of this new universe, and trying to fight his way out of it.

I began walking down the road, right in the centre where the lanes met. Black hair, black dress; the sun was almost down, and I was a night-thing too. I made a low sound in my throat to see if anything would answer. When no response came I cackled, and somewhere in the distance a bird shrieked.

Crepuscular. I said the word under my breath. Something was coming, that much was certain. Something was coming, and I was walking straight into it.

Acknowledgements

Some of these stories have previously appeared or are forthcoming in literary journals, magazines or anthologies, or have won or placed in competitions:

'The Leopard Next Door' was a winner in the 2015 Nat. Brut Flash Fiction Contest. It appeared in *Nat. Brut* in July 2016.

'Tongue-Tied' won the 2019 Iowa Review Award in Fiction, and appeared in the December 2019 edition of *The Iowa Review*.

'Powerful Owl' was runner-up in the 2018 Bristol Short Story Prize, and appeared in the *Bristol Short Story Prize Anthology* vol. 11.

'Arm's Length' appeared in *Landmarks* (2017), an anthology published by Spineless Wonders.

'Harbour' was shortlisted for the 2017 Commonwealth Short Story Prize.

An earlier version of 'Monstera' ('Communion') was shortlisted for the 2018 Manchester Fiction Prize.

'Frogs' Legs' was a finalist in the 2018 Robert J. DeMott Short Prose Contest and was published in *Quarter After Eight* vol. 25.

'Hold Your Fire' was published in *Granta 151: Membranes* (Spring 2020).

'Blood Bag' was longlisted for the 2018 SmokeLong Quarterly Award for Flash Fiction.

'The Drydown' was shortlisted for the 2016 Margaret River Press Short Story Competition. It appeared in that year's prize anthology, *Shibboleth and Other Stories*.

'Exchange' was published in *Flash: The International Short-Short Story Magazine*, Issue 7.2 (October 2014).

'Joyriders' was published in *The Big Issue*'s 2019 Fiction Edition. It was also shortlisted for the 2019 Bath Short Story Award, and appeared in the 2019 prize anthology.

'Break Character' was commended in the 2018 Elizabeth Jolley Short Story Prize, and was published in *Australian Book Review* online in November 2018.

'Animus' was runner-up in the 2017 ELLE Australia Writing Competition, and appeared in the February 2018 issue of *ELLE* Australia.

About the Author

Chloe Wilson's 'Hold Your Fire' was published in *Granta 151: Membranes* (Spring 2020); 'Tongue-Tied' won the 2019 Iowa Review Fiction Prize, judged by Rebecca Makkai; and 'Harbour' was shortlisted for the 2017 Commonwealth Short Story Prize. She is also the author of two poetry collections, *The Mermaid Problem* and *Not Fox Nor Axe*, which was shortlisted for the Kenneth Slessor Prize for Poetry and the Judith Wright Calanthe Award. Her work has appeared in numerous publications. Chloe is a former *Voiceworks* Poetry Editor and holds a PhD in Creative Writing from the University of Melbourne, where she currently lives.